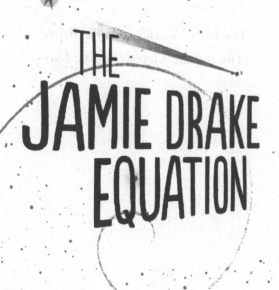

THE
JAMIE DRAKE
EQUATION

ALSO BY CHRISTOPHER EDGE

The Many Worlds of Albie Bright
The Infinite Lives of Maisie Day

THE
JAMIE DRAKE
EQUATION

Christopher Edge

A YEARLING BOOK

Text copyright © 2017, 2018 by Christopher Edge
Cover art copyright © 2018 by Jamey Christoph
Interior illustrations on pp. 58 and 90 copyright © 2017 by Spike Gerrell

All rights reserved. Published in the United States by Yearling,
an imprint of Random House Children's Books, a division of
Penguin Random House LLC, New York. Originally published in the
United Kingdom in paperback and in slightly different form by
Nosy Crow, London, in 2017, and subsequently published in hardcover in the
United States by Delacorte Press, an imprint of Random House Children's Books,
a division of Penguin Random House LLC, New York, in 2018.

Yearling and the jumping horse design are registered trademarks
of Penguin Random House LLC.

Visit us on the Web! rhcbooks.com

Educators and librarians, for a variety of teaching tools,
visit us at RHTeachersLibrarians.com

The Library of Congress has cataloged
the hardcover edition of this work as follows:
Names: Edge, Christopher, author.
Title: The Jamie Drake equation / Christopher Edge.
Description: First American edition. | New York : Delacorte Press, 2018. |
"Originally published in paperback by Nosy Crow, London, in 2017."
Summary: Jamie has a close encounter with an alien who tells him his father,
an astronaut on a mission at the International Space Station,
is in trouble and needs Jamie's help.
Identifiers: LCCN 2017028503 (print) | LCCN 2017040441 (ebook) |
ISBN 978-1-5247-1362-1 (ebook) | ISBN 978-1-5247-1361-4 (trade hardcover)
Subjects: | CYAC: Life on other planets—Fiction. | Extraterrestrial beings—
Fiction. | Astronauts—Fiction. | Family life—England—Fiction. | Fathers and
sons—Fiction. | England—Fiction. | Science fiction.
Classification: LCC PZ7.E2265 (ebook) | LCC PZ7.E2265 Jam 2018 (print) |
DDC [Fic]—dc23

ISBN 978-1-5247-1364-5 (pbk.)

Printed in the United States of America

First Yearling Edition 2019

FOR CHRISSIE, ALEX, AND JOSIE

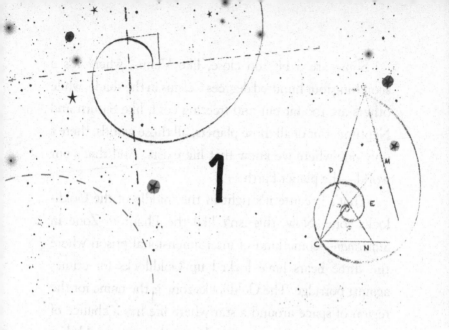

1

YOU'RE SUPPOSED TO START A STORY AT THE BEGINNING, right? The thing is, knowing exactly *when* that is can be kind of difficult. I mean, I could start this story with how the solar system was formed about four and a half billion years ago. That was when the center of a huge cloud of gas and dust that was spinning in space got superhot and turned into a star, but *this* story really got started way before that.

It's all about putting things in the right order. That's how the solar system got going, as scientists know. Once the sun was formed, the rest of the dust and stuff got stuck together to make the planets and moons, and since then they've just kept spinning around the sun, year after year.

Some are a bit too close, like Venus, where it's a scorching four hundred degrees Celsius in the shade, while others are too far out and freezing cold, like Saturn and Neptune. But of all those planets, all those worlds, there's only one where we know that life exists. And that's our world—the planet Earth.

That's because it's right in the middle of the Goldilocks zone. Now, this isn't like the Phantom Zone in *Superman*—some kind of interdimensional prison where the three bears have locked up Goldilocks for crimes against porridge. The Goldilocks zone is the name for the region of space around a star where life has a chance of existing. Somewhere not too hot and not too cold, but just right. And in our solar system, Earth has this spot completely to itself.

It's a bit like my family, really. There's Mom, Dad, Charlie, and me, Jamie Drake. Dad's the star in our family's solar system because he's an astronaut. Everyone at school knows his name, and he's been on TV loads of times talking about his latest space mission. He's kind of like Captain Kirk crossed with Han Solo but cooler because he's a real person.

To be fair, I reckon Mom's the star too because she keeps everything running smoothly when Dad's not around, so that just leaves Charlie and me in the Goldilocks zone.

It used to be that I had this spot totally to myself, but

then four years ago Mom and Dad told me I was going to have a baby sister. At first I wasn't too sure, but then Mom explained that tons of people think the perfect family has four people in it, so by adding a little sister, our family was going to be just the right size, and when baby Charlotte was born, I kind of had to agree.

Our family's solar system is now perfectly balanced. Mom + Dad = Me + Charlie.

Now, if you move any part of the real solar system, then the whole thing goes to pieces, with planets crashing into each other or flying off into the depths of space. Everything has to be in just the right place for Earth to keep spinning safely around the sun. So with Dad four hundred kilometers above our heads on the International Space Station, I'm keeping a close eye on things at home in case any bits of the Drake family solar system start to wobble.

So far, everything's okay. In fact, Mom and Dad were arguing a lot before he blasted off into orbit, and I think having this break has just made them realize how much they love each other after all. And in ten days' time, Dad will land safely back on Earth, and our family can get back to normal. It's just a shame he's going to miss my birthday on Friday.

That's the day of his space walk. The day the human race launches its first mission to the stars in search of alien life. I hope he hasn't forgotten to get me a present.

3

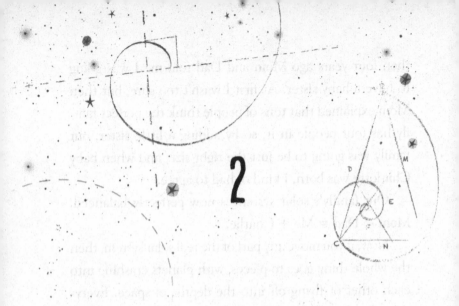

2

THIS WEEK IS SPACE WEEK IN SCHOOL. EVERY CLASS IS LEARN-
ing all about my dad's mission. When I took the register
back to the school office yesterday, I spotted Class Three
making models of the International Space Station out of
tinfoil and toilet-paper rolls, and then on the way back to
my own class I bumped into this little kid who was dressed
up like a baby alien. I nearly jumped out of my skin in
surprise. He was wearing a homemade space suit, his face
painted bright green with sparkly deely-boppers sticking
out of his frizz of black hair.

"I know who you are," he said, looking up at me
openmouthed, his eyes wide with wonder. "Your dad's
a *spaceman*."

4

"That's right," I said, feeling pretty cool that my fame had spread all the way to the first grade. "I'm Jamie Drake."

This kid starts jigging up and down with excitement, his deely-boppers bouncing around wildly. Then he asks me the question I get asked at least three times a day.

"How does your dad go to the bathroom in space?"

Up on the International Space Station, everything is weightless, so my dad just floats around and can even fly like a superhero. But all anyone ever wants to know is how Dad goes to the bathroom.

I'm in sixth grade. This means that we get to do all the serious educational stuff about my dad's mission. This week we're learning about alien worlds, interstellar travel, and nanotechnology. Right now our teacher, Mrs. Solomon, is writing our Space Week homework on the whiteboard.

INVENT AN ALIEN

"Is there anybody out there?" Mrs. Solomon asks, turning back to face us with a grin. She points up at the sky outside our classroom window. "Do aliens exist, or are we all alone in the universe?"

Sitting next to me, Minty pokes her elbow into my ribs.

"Course they do," she whispers. "I've seen them on YouTube."

Minty's real name is Araminta, and she used to go to a posh private school, but then her dad got sent to prison for some big bank robbery and she ended up here at Austen Park Primary. Sometimes I think the police got the wrong member of the family and they should've locked Minty up instead, especially when she keeps on poking me in the ribs. I wish I didn't have to sit next to her, but Mrs. Solomon seems to think we should become friends just because we're both the new kids at school.

Minty watches all these zany YouTube videos made by weirdos who wear tinfoil on their heads. One showed a rubber dummy that was supposed to be an alien being sliced to pieces by these doctors dressed in space suits. It was obviously a fake, but Minty swore that it was a real-life alien autopsy.

"This Friday," Mrs. Solomon continues, glancing down as she taps at the laptop on her desk, "Jamie's dad, Commander Dan Drake, is launching a mission to the stars to search for alien life. Let's take a look at this video to find out more about his mission."

Next to the whiteboard, the flat-screen display flickers to life. There I see a picture of my dad dressed in his astronaut gear, flanked by the rest of the ISS crew. The butterflies in my stomach start to flutter as this frozen picture slowly dissolves to reveal an image of a strange-looking satellite shaped like a silver ball flying high above Earth. Then an incredibly deep voice like the one you hear on trailers for the latest blockbuster movies starts to rumble from the speakers.

"From the launch of the first satellite in 1957, the human race has endeavored to explore every corner of the solar system in which we live. From planetary landings to solar surveys, the knowledge we have gained has helped us to understand our unique place in the universe. Now it is time for the human race to take our next step and begin to explore our galaxy."

As the voice speaks, spectacular photographs fill the screen. I see the dusty red mountains of Mars stretching out under a butterscotch sky, Jupiter's swirling storms, and the ice rings of Saturn. Images of Mercury, Venus, Uranus, and Neptune, each world so beautiful and strange. Then these pictures start to speed up, the planets flashing by in a blur of colors—yellow, red, brown, blue, and green—before dissolving to reveal a photograph of the sun. This looks like a blazing ball of fire, glowing red flares arcing from its surface into space.

"Our sun is only one star out of the two hundred billion stars that make up our galaxy, the Milky Way," the voice announces. "Until now, the great distances between these stars has kept the possibility of interstellar travel out of humanity's grasp, but with advances in microelectronics, nanotechnology, and laser engineering, at last the human race can reach for the stars."

The screen fades to black, and for a second, I think the film is finished, but then the camera pans to reveal another satellite in orbit high above Earth. This one looks like a flower, an array of futuristic solar panels curving to create a spiral of petals in space. At the base of this strange satellite, there's a sleek silver module with an air lock at the far end—the HabZone module of the Lux Aeterna launch platform.

"Led by Commander Dan Drake," the voice continues, "the crew of the International Space Station are now making their preparations for the final phase of the Lux Aeterna mission. Construction of the orbital launch platform is now complete, and on Friday the third of November at oh-eight-hundred hours GMT, Commander Drake will use the Advanced Manned Maneuvering Unit to travel from the ISS to the higher orbit of the Lux Aeterna launch platform to perform final checks on the Light Swarm probes. Each of these nano-spacecraft is the size of a postage stamp and weighs less than a sheet of paper. When Commander Drake fires the Lux Aeterna's one-hundred-gigawatt laser array, the sails on board the Light Swarm probes will catch this laser beam and then accelerate to more than seventy-five percent of the speed of light."

Dad told me *Lux Aeterna* is a Latin phrase that means "eternal light," which is a pretty cool name for a giant space laser.

On the screen a swarm of silver kites floats free from the heart of the flower. Inside the satellite's spiral of solar panels, I see an inner ring of glowing red lights—the launch platform's laser array. As I watch, these red lights suddenly shoot out to form a single beam, this red laser light striking the space kites and accelerating them to the stars.

"Launched on their interstellar journey, the Light Swarm probes will travel to a star called Tau Ceti. Located one hundred and eight trillion kilometers from Earth, Tau Ceti is orbited by a system of five planets with at least one of these worlds located within the star's 'Goldilocks zone,' where liquid water—and life—could exist."

Strange new planets now fill the screen, worlds of ice and oceans, burning blue in the depths of space.

"Traveling at 299,792 kilometers per second, it takes twelve years for the light from Tau Ceti to reach us here on Earth. At this great distance it would take a conventional spacecraft one hundred thousand years to reach this star system, but traveling near light speed, the Light Swarm probes will complete their journey to Tau Ceti in approximately fifteen years. Once there, the robotic probes will use onboard cameras, sensors, and communications systems to search for alien life, using the same laser-pulse technology to beam their findings back to Earth, to reach us here in another fifteen years. Thanks to the efforts of Commander Dan Drake and the ISS crew, within your lifetime the human race might finally discover the answer to the eternal question, 'Are we alone in the universe?'"

As the screen fades to black again, this time for good, everyone starts clapping and cheering. I can't stop myself from blushing, knowing that they're cheering for my dad. I feel so proud of him, but strangely, I can't help feeling a tiny bit jealous too. Everything revolves around the fact that Dad's an astronaut—where we live, where we go on vacation, and now even my lessons in school. Sometimes I wish I didn't have to share him with the world.

"Are we alone in the universe?" Beaming excitedly, Mrs. Solomon repeats the question. "That's what I want you to think about, Class Six."

Turning back to the whiteboard, our teacher takes aim with her laser pointer to underline our homework task.

INVENT AN ALIEN

"Imagine the planets the Light Swarm probes might discover orbiting Tau Ceti. What strange alien creatures could they find there? For your homework, I want you to invent your own alien species. Think about the kind of world that it's from. Does this world have jungles or deserts, or might it be some kind of water world? How will this affect the type of alien you invent? Will it need tentacles instead of arms and legs like you and me? Maybe it could fly like a bird through clouds of ice and dust? Use your imagination to answer the following questions: where will this alien live, what might it eat, and how could it communicate?"

Everyone starts talking at once—the whole class bubbling with excitement about the idea of dreaming up their own alien life-form. Minty turns to me with a quizzical look on her face.

"So what will your dad do if he meets an alien up there?" she asks. "Has he got some kind of ray gun to blast it to bits before it starts eating him? Aliens just love the taste of human flesh."

Kind of grossed out, I quickly shake my head.

"My dad's not going to Tau Ceti," I tell her, speaking slowly to make sure Minty understands, seeing as she seems to have completely missed the point of the video. "He's just going to do a space walk to launch the Light Swarm probes. They're the ones that are heading to the stars in search of alien life."

11

Minty pulls a face like I'm the stupid one.

"Yeah, but that doesn't mean that some Martian won't fly past when your dad's on his space walk and make a meat feast pizza out of him."

As you can see, Minty is seriously annoying.

"My dad's on the International Space Station," I say. "Not the menu of some intergalactic Pizza Hut."

I'm just about to add that Martians don't actually exist when our teacher claps her hands together.

"I'm so pleased to hear you all so excited about your homework," Mrs. Solomon says, raising her voice so she can be heard over the hubbub. "And I look forward to seeing your presentations about the weird and wonderful aliens you've invented on Thursday. If you like, you can even dress up as your alien creation! But right now we need to practice another essential skill that all astronauts need."

She turns back to the whiteboard, erasing the homework task and writing the word "EQUATIONS" there instead.

"It's time to study for your math test tomorrow."

Everyone groans, including me. It's true—you do need to be a total math genius to make it as an astronaut. That's why I always get my dad to help me with my math homework. But since he went into orbit, my marks have taken a bit of a nosedive. I mean, we get to chat on the phone most days and have a family video conference once a week, but I don't want to waste this talking about sums when Dad's floating in space.

As Mrs. Solomon hands out our revision sheets, I look down at the list of equations with a sinking feeling. I wish Dad were here to help me.

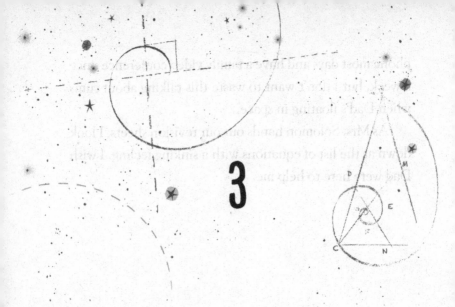

3

AFTER LUNCH MRS. SOLOMON GETS US TO TEST OUT THE theory of gravity in the gym by dropping balls from the top of the agility tables. It's like an experiment that this old Italian guy called Galileo did when he dropped cannon-balls off the Leaning Tower of Pisa. She gets us lined up holding different types of balls: basketballs, cricket balls, tennis balls, and golf balls. She says that even though you might think that the heaviest balls would fall fastest and hit the ground first, gravity accelerates them at the same rate, so the balls all hit the ground at the same time.

That's the theory, anyway, but then Minty pulled a Ping-Pong ball out of her pocket, and when we dropped the balls at the same time, Minty's ball hit the ground after everyone else's. Mrs. Solomon said this was because the Ping-Pong ball is very light, so it was slowed by air resistance, but I just think that the theory of gravity doesn't work when Minty's around.

Stepping out of the school gates at the end of the day, I hear the beep of a horn. Turning around, my heart sinks when I see Granddad Neil instead of Mom waiting to pick me up. He leans out the driver's window of his van.

"Come on, slowpoke!" he yells. "That crossing guard says I can't park here." Dressed in her luminous yellow jacket, Mrs. Bagwell shouts angrily back at Granddad.

"No, you can't—you're a danger to the children crossing. You shouldn't even be allowed on the road in that . . . thing!"

Back in the 1980s, Granddad used to be the lead singer of a rock band called Death Panda, until a problem with his ears forced him to retire. He still drives his old tour van, and through the windshield I can see Charlie crammed into her car seat in the back, waving an inflatable guitar above her head. But that's not what makes the crossing guard tut as she glares at Granddad's bad parking. It's the huge mural that's painted on the side of the van.

This shows a cartoon of a panda riding on the back of a nuclear missile heading straight for the sun. It's a pretty

15

eye-catching picture. This was the front cover of Death Panda's first album, *Global Warming? This Means War!*

As I reluctantly climb inside the van, the rest of my class streaming out from the school gates, I hear Aaron Johnson shout out, "Nice wheels, Jamie!" Everyone starts laughing. I duck down in the passenger seat to try and make myself invisible, but this doesn't work, as Charlie starts bashing me on the head with the blow-up guitar. Still leaning out the window, Granddad raises his fist in the air, his index and little finger extended to form the sign of the horns. As he salutes the school with this heavy-metal hand gesture, I sink down farther into my seat.

"Do you want to give any of your friends a ride home?" Granddad Neil asks, flicking his long gray ponytail back as he squeezes his stomach behind the steering wheel. "There's plenty of room."

Fastening my seat belt, I quickly shake my head. Having a dad who's an astronaut is really cool, but Granddad is a serious embarrassment.

"No, it's okay—I just want to go home."

"Right you are, then." With a shrug, Granddad turns the key in the ignition. "Let's hit the road."

A tsunami of noise erupts from the speakers, almost drowning out the engine as it roars to life.

"I'm a Love Missile, baby—and I shoot to thrill!"

I quickly jam my fingers into my ears, trying to block out the worst of the sound. In the back, Charlie squeals with delight, whirling the inflatable guitar around her head again as the thunderous sound of Death Panda rings out.

"The temperature is rising as I go for the kill."

The van lurches away from the pavement, the crossing guard flattening herself against the school gates as twin guitars squeal from the speakers. Glancing back in the side mirror, I can see her angrily shaking her stop sign before Granddad turns the corner and she disappears from view.

Home for us is actually Granddad's house. Before Dad was an astronaut, he was in the Royal Air Force, and we just used to live on whichever base he was posted to. Mom and Dad never got around to buying a house—most of the time they just rented a studio for Mom where she could make her sculptures and stuff while we lived in family quarters.

We moved a lot anyway as the planes Dad flew got bigger and bigger. I went to three different schools before I was eight years old as he learned how to fly helicopters, spy planes, and fighter jets. Then Dad decided he wanted to become an astronaut, and that was when we really started racking up the air miles.

Most of his basic astronaut training took place in

Germany, and I had to go to an international school in Cologne. Then there was underwater training in Florida so Dad could learn how to survive in an extreme environment, while I tried out the high-g rides at Disney World, before we headed to Moscow, where Dad learned to space walk and I learned that I don't really like Russian food. That was where Charlie popped out, so her birth certificate says she was born in Star City. This is the name of the place near Moscow where all the astronauts and their families live while they're finishing their training. My birth certificate just says I was born in Swindon.

So anyway, after Dad blasted off for the International Space Station, Mom brought me and Charlie back home to Britain, and we moved in with Granddad Neil. I don't know why we couldn't get our own house, but Mom said that Granddad would help look after us while she got back to work. I told Mom I didn't need any looking after, but we still moved into Granddad's house. He bought it when he was big in the '80s, and since Grandma left him and moved to the States with her new boyfriend, he's been living there on his own. Now Mom's turned her old attic bedroom into an art studio and is up there most of the time working on her new sculpture.

She's in the kitchen when we get home, though, drinking a cup of tea in her paint-spattered smock.

Charlie runs toward her with a happy squeal, shrieking with delight as Mom scoops her up and spins her in the air.

"I'm a spaceman!" she cries.

Mom rolls her eyes.

"You mean a spacewoman," Mom says as she brings Charlie back down to earth. "Don't forget, girls can be astronauts too."

Then she gives me a smile as I shrug my backpack off my shoulders and set it down on the kitchen table.

"How was school?" she asks.

"Fine," I reply, pulling out my homework folder. "I've just got to study for this math test tomorrow."

From the back garden comes an earsplitting squeal of feedback, and my shoulders sag as I realize what this means. Even though Granddad's rock-star days are over, he still likes to go out to the barn to play his guitar. Very, very loudly. There goes my chance of studying in peace.

Seeing the pained expression on my face, Mom quickly shakes her head.

"Don't start studying now," she says, raising her voice as the sound of a crunching guitar chord rings out and Charlie starts dancing around the kitchen. "Why don't you get some fresh air first? I'll make sure Granddad finishes practicing by six, and you can pick us all up some fish and chips on your way back."

Mom pulls out some money and pushes it into my hand.

Grateful for the chance to escape, I quickly shove the notes into my pocket along with my revision work sheet. As the deafening *kerrang* of another guitar chord shakes the kitchen window, I head for the door and the one place where I'm guaranteed some peace and quiet.

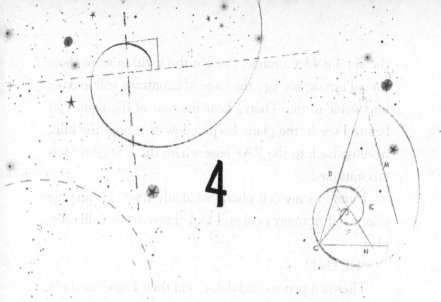

4

FROM UP HERE ON BEACON HILL YOU CAN SEE EVERYTHING.
The whole village is spread out below me like a Google
map. There's Granddad's house, the long backyard with
the barn at the bottom on the edge of the wild meadows.
Luckily, I can't hear his guitar playing from here. Then
over there is my school, Austen Park Primary, its green
playing fields surrounded by the new housing estate.
The houses look like little boxes, and with my finger and
thumb I pinch and drag out the empty air, trying to zoom
in to imagine what kind of family I'd find inside each one.
I bet they wouldn't have an annoying granddad like mine.

The sun is starting to dip on the horizon, turning

the sky a golden orange. I've got the revision work sheet spread out on my lap, the page of equations still looking impossible to me. Then I hear the roar of the fighter jet before I see it, the plane keeping low as it hugs the hills, heading back to the RAF base where the US fighter jets are stationed.

I jump as my cell phone suddenly rings. Fishing my phone out from my pocket, I look down at the caller display.

"Hi, Dad."

There's a two-second delay, and then I hear my dad's voice on the other end of the line.

"Hi, Jamie. I just called your mom and Charlie at home, but I couldn't get hold of you, so I wanted to check you were okay."

Dad's kind of amazing. He's not even on this planet, but he's still making sure I'm all right.

"Where are you, son?"

"Up on Beacon Hill," I say. "I wanted a bit of peace and quiet for a while. Granddad's practicing his guitar again."

Dad laughs.

"Beacon Hill's probably the only place in Bramsfield where you can't hear Neil's guitar. I used to take your mom up there when we first started going out."

Mom and Dad both grew up in this village. They

started going out when they were still at school and have been together ever since. All the newspapers say it's so romantic.

"There used to be an observatory up there at the top of the hill," Dad continues. "Your mom and I would go in on their open evenings and look up at the stars. When I looked through the telescope, it seemed as though the moon was close enough to touch. I could even see the spot where Neil Armstrong took his first step. I think that's what made me want to fly a spaceship, but I'm stuck here whizzing around in low Earth orbit instead. In fact, I'm heading over you right now, Jamie. Give us a wave."

I look up, my eyes scanning the horizon until I see the familiar glint of the ISS—a silver streak in the darkening sky. Dad showed me how to spot this before he went up into space. It looks just like a fast-moving plane but without any flashing lights, and because the ISS is so high up, it doesn't make a sound. Dad promised me that whenever he was flying straight overhead, he'd always keep an eye out for me.

"I can see you, Dad," I say, lifting my hand to wave at this shooting star.

"Me too, son," he replies, his voice as clear in my ear as if he were sitting next to me and not four hundred kilometers above my head.

There's a moment of silence as I try to work out what

23

to say next. When Dad's at home, I can talk to him about anything—all the funny things that happen at school, any problems I've got with my homework, what we're going to do together on the weekend. Everything I'm thinking about and all my worries too.

There's so much I want to tell him now. How I wish he were home for my birthday, how living with Granddad is driving me mad, and how I can't stop worrying about his space walk on Friday. But when you've only got a few minutes to talk, it's hard to fit everything in.

Then I hear a long beeping tone in the background, like a phone that's been left off the hook.

"Are you still there, Dad?" I ask.

I hear the echo of my own voice on the line, and then Dad's voice cuts back in.

"I'm going to have to go, Jamie. This is something I need to check out."

"Is everything okay?" I ask, panicking at the thought of anything going wrong up there. From meteor strikes to toxic leaks, Dad has explained to me all the different dangers he could face on the ISS. In an extreme emergency, the astronauts have to take shelter in the Soyuz capsule that's connected to the space station in case they need to make a quick escape.

"No need to worry, son," he replies. "It's just a caution alert. Probably some computer system's gone offline."

As he speaks, the beeping tone suddenly stops.

"There you go," he says. "Panic over. I just need to find out what this alert was about, and then I can inform Mission Control. I'll speak to you tomorrow on our family video call."

The ISS is dipping low on the horizon now, giving me one last glimpse before it disappears.

"Bye, Jamie."

"Bye, Dad."

And then he's gone, traveling around the world in a tin can at over twenty-seven thousand kilometers per hour.

I'm nearly out of breath by the time I reach the very top of Beacon Hill, my shadow lengthening as the last rays of the sun leach out of the sky. I can't stop myself from shivering. I should've brought a jacket. Mom is probably expecting me back about now, but I don't want to go home yet. I want to see the observatory that Dad mentioned first.

If it was here when my dad was a teenager, then it must be well out of date by now. They put telescopes up into space nowadays so that astronomers can look farther and farther out into the universe. I glance up at the darkening sky, clouds now starting to appear on the horizon as daylight fades away. You wouldn't be able to see much from here.

Then I see it, half hidden behind a bank of trees, a squat redbrick building topped with a white dome-shaped roof. The walls of the building are half covered in ivy and shrubs, making it blend in with the woodland that surrounds it, and as I get closer I can see coils of barbed wire sitting below the lip of the dome, its white paint peeling in places and mottled with a greenish tint. The observatory looks abandoned, the only clue to its former life the rectangular slit in the side of the dome, left open to the sky.

I reach a rusting chain-link fence, the battered red-and-white sign that's fixed to this warning:

PRIVATE PROPERTY
TRESPASSERS WILL BE PROSECUTED

But less than a meter to the left I spot a gap between the fence post and a padlocked gate, the chain hanging so loose that it's easy for me to squeeze through.

Up close, the observatory looks even more derelict, its curved redbrick walls crumbling in places, the chunks of rubble almost lost among the weeds. It doesn't look like anyone has been here for years. There are no windows, and as I skirt the edge of the building in search of a door,

I wonder what might be left inside. Maybe the telescope is still working and I'll be able to catch a close-up of Dad on his next orbit in ninety minutes' time. If I could just find a way in . . .

Then I see something that stops me in my tracks. Silhouetted against the setting sun, it looks like a robot riding on top of a giant techno-spider. It's nearly twice my height, its four metal legs extended and planted in the ground, while the satellite dish head is pointing to the stars. On its sleek white body I can see a bright blue logo:

★ L.O.G.S.

Unlike the crumbling observatory, this looks like it's just fallen off the back of a spaceship. I step closer, peering at the strange machine to try and work out exactly what it is.

That's when I feel the shotgun press between my shoulder blades.

"Don't move," a woman's voice growls, "or I'll let you have it."

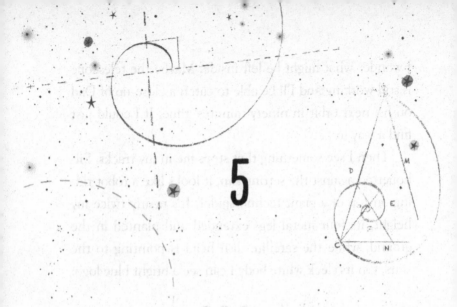

5

I WALK SLOWLY UP THE STAIRS THAT HUG THE CURVING WALL, my eyes straining against the gloom that lurks inside the observatory. The concrete steps leading up to the next level are coated with pigeon droppings, and I have to pick my path carefully to make sure I don't slip. It's cold in here, but despite the chill, I can feel a bead of sweat sliding down my face as the barrel of the shotgun pressed into my back pushes me forward again.

"Keep moving," the woman tells me as we reach the top of the stairs. "In there."

Trying to keep down the taste of sick that's bubbling up in my throat, I push open the door in front of me and step through into a huge dimly lit room. The floor is smeared with a thick layer of dust, but the curved walls are filled with banks of electronic equipment. There are rows of computers that look like they haven't been upgraded since the 1980s, the chunky monitors and keyboards all covered in the same thick layer of dust. Multicolored cables snake between tall gray cabinets, their insides crammed with reels and dials. An eerie silence hangs in the air, but it's what I can see in the middle of the room that makes me catch my breath.

Mounted on a towering base that stretches six meters high is a huge telescope. It looks like a space rocket, the long white tube as thick as a tree trunk and studded with rivets, gears, and levers, pointing up at a forty-five-degree angle. On one side of the tower, metal stairs spiral upward to reach a chair that's mounted on a set of rails beside the bottom end of the telescope. And at the other end, the telescope lens looks out of the rectangular slit, the rusting dome still open to the stars that are starting to come out overhead.

A prod in my back reminds me that I haven't come here for stargazing.

"Over there," the woman says, pushing me toward a long desk in front of one of the banks of defunct computers. "Empty your pockets."

I haven't even seen her face, but with a shotgun shoved in my back, I'm not in a position to argue.

Reaching into my pockets, I empty them out onto the

29

table in front of me: my house keys, a packet of Starmix, my revision work sheet, and the money Mom gave me.

"Everything," she growls.

With a trembling hand, I take out my cell phone and lay this down next to the rest. There goes any chance of calling the police. My brain starts to cycle through what will happen next—every possibility I imagine is even worse than the last. She's probably some serial killer who roams abandoned buildings looking for kids to kill. Why didn't I stay at home?

I can still feel the gun, and from over my shoulder I glimpse the shape of a shadow leaning forward. . . .

I hear a click and almost jump out of my skin, waiting for my life to flash before my eyes. But instead of a shot, I see the lamp on the desk flicker to life.

"Sit down," she tells me, the strange shadow of her shotgun pointing to the chair on the other side of the desk.

I sit down. The desk lamp is shining straight into my face, almost blinding me.

"What are you doing sneaking around here?"

I squint up at my questioner, trying to see past the blotches forming in front of my eyes. Instead of the menacing killer of my imagination, a middle-aged woman wearing a pink cardigan over a floral dress is standing there, her black hair twisted into braids. In her hands, she's holding a telescope, its eyepiece pointing straight at me like the barrel of a gun.

The realization hits like a bullet. This is what she had pressed into my back the whole time. I've been taken prisoner with a telescope.

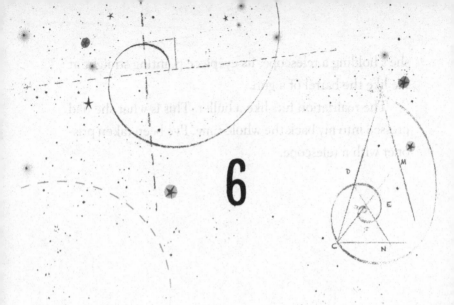

6

"I THOUGHT YOU HAD A GUN," I PROTEST, STARTING TO GET
up out of the seat.

"I've got a doctorate in astrophysics and a black belt in karate," the woman replies, poking me hard in the chest with her telescope. "So sit down before I knock your block off."

Now, it might not be as big as the one pointing up out of the dome, but the end of this telescope still feels rather painful as she prods it into my chest. I sit back down.

"What are you doing here?" she asks again, staring sternly at me.

"My dad told me there used to be an observatory on

Beacon Hill," I tell her, glancing around nervously at the old computer equipment. "I thought I'd come and take a look myself. I thought this place was abandoned. I didn't think anyone was still working here."

"It's private property. Didn't you see the sign?"

"No," I lie, suddenly remembering the warning about trespassers being prosecuted. "My dad said that this place used to be open to the public. I can see now that it's all shut down, but what's that weird robot thing you've got outside? The rest of this place is old, but that thing looks brand-new."

The woman ignores my question, suspicion still shining in her eyes.

"Who is your dad? Why's he told you to come poking around here?"

"He didn't tell me to come poking around." I start to pick my things up off the desk. "And now that I know that this place is out of bounds, I'll get out of your way."

"But who is he?" She snatches my phone out of my hand. "I'll call him up now to find out why he's sent you to spy on me."

"He didn't send me to spy on you," I repeat, raising my voice in exasperation. "And you can't call my dad."

"Why not?" she says, peering intently at the phone screen as she scrolls through the numbers in my contacts. "Scared I'm going to find out the truth?"

"Because he's in space," I snap. "My dad's Commander Dan Drake."

The woman stares at me for a second, her forehead creasing in a frown, and then she laughs out loud.

"I *knew* I recognized your face from somewhere," she replies. "You were in the newspaper with your dad—you and your mom and your little sister too—'The Space Family Drake.'"

I wince as I remember the headline. Before Dad went into orbit, the *Sunday Times* did a story about our whole family, talking about Dad's mission and how we felt about him going up into space. For the photograph, the newspaper thought it would be a good idea if Charlie and me dressed up as aliens. Charlie loved it and kept on hitting Dad over the head with the lightsaber the photographer gave her, but when you're in sixth grade, it's a bit embarrassing to have to wear pointy ears.

The woman slowly lowers her telescope, and for the first time, I start to think I might get out of here in one piece.

"What's your name?" she asks.

"Jamie," I reply. "Jamie Drake."

"That's right," the woman says, clicking her fingers as if pulling the memory back into focus. "In that photo with your dad you were dressed like a mini Mr. Spock out of *Star Trek*, and your sister made the cutest little Yoda."

34

The pointy ears were embarrassing, but at least I didn't have to paint my face green like Charlie.

"But this still doesn't explain why you're trespassing," she continues, a trace of suspicion remaining in her voice. "What were you trying to do? Take a peek through the telescope at your dad up on the ISS?"

I shake my head. I might as well tell her the truth.

"I just thought it might be nice and quiet up here." And then I tell her about how I need to study for my math test tomorrow, how Granddad Neil still thinks he's a rock star, and how it's kind of hard to concentrate when all you can hear is the squeal of a heavy-metal guitar.

"So you thought you'd come and disturb my work instead?" the woman says with a frown.

I look around at the ancient equipment stacked haphazardly on metal racks and filling gray cabinets, all covered in a thick layer of dust. It doesn't look like any of this stuff has been used in years. The only thing that looks brand-new in here is a laptop that's set up at the other end of this desk. An external modem is plugged into one of its USB ports, the bright blue logo on this reading ★ L.O.G.S.

"What is your work?" I ask, still trying to understand exactly what she's doing here.

"Well, like, duh," the woman replies, gesturing toward the huge telescope. "Isn't it obvious? I'm an astronomer."

There's the hint of a smile on her face as she hands me back my phone. "I'm Professor Forster."

Professor Forster doesn't look how I imagined an astronomer would look. She doesn't seem to act like one either. I thought they all had gray hair and spectacles and spoke in posh voices. Professor Forster is . . . *different*.

"So what exactly are you looking for?" I ask, glancing up to see clouds scudding across the rectangle of sky still visible through the roof of the dome. "I mean, you can't see much from here."

"I'm waiting for the stars to give up their secrets," Professor Forster replies mysteriously. "I'm looking for a sign."

She perches on the desk next to me, tilting her head to one side as she fixes me with a quizzical stare.

"Have you ever wondered if we're all alone, Jamie?"

I glance nervously over my shoulder. Under the observatory dome the banks of electronic equipment lurk silently in the dim light, while the door leading to the stairs stands empty.

"I think we are," I reply, shifting uncomfortably in my seat. "I can't see anybody else here."

"I mean in the *universe!*" the astronomer explodes, making me nearly jump out of my seat. "What are the chances that Earth is the only planet where intelligent life exists?"

"So you're looking for aliens?" I say, quickly realizing

my mistake. I think about Dad getting ready for his space walk on Friday. "Has this got something to do with my dad's mission? He's launching the Light Swarm probes to search for signs of alien life."

The astronomer shakes her head, a superior smile now playing across her lips.

"My work is a little more unofficial than Commander Drake's mission," she replies. "But, dare I say it, it has a much greater chance of success. Your father is sending those tiny spacecraft to Tau Ceti, a single star located twelve light-years away. But the Milky Way measures one hundred thousand light-years across and contains more than two hundred billion stars." She flings her arms wide with a flourish. "I'm searching the whole galaxy for a signal."

"What kind of a signal?" I ask, kind of annoyed that she thinks she's got a better plan than my dad.

To answer my question, Professor Forster picks up a pen and grabs hold of my revision work sheet.

"We've been sending our own signals for about a hundred years," she explains, scrawling a circle in the space at the bottom of the page. In the middle of this circle, she writes a single word: "EARTH." "Every radio and TV transmission that the human race has ever broadcast leaks out of Earth's atmosphere and travels into space at the speed of light." She draws a set of wavy lines radiating out of the circle in every direction. "If any of our near neighbors in the Milky Way are listening out for these radio and TV signals, they'll be able to tell that there's intelligent life here on Earth."

Professor Forster now scribbles two asterisks on the work sheet, one close to the circle and the other near the edge of the page. She points her pen at the first of these.

"Proxima Centauri is only four and a quarter light-years from Earth, so any aliens there might be watching an episode of *Doctor Who*." Professor Forster now moves her pen so it's pointing to the second, more distant star. "While any alien worlds orbiting 16 Cygni, a star system seventy light-years away, will have only just heard about the end of the Second World War."

I imagine a real-life alien sitting down to watch *Doctor Who*. I just hope it's not a Dalek.

Professor Forster now starts scribbling new sets of wavy lines radiating out from both of the asterisks on the page.

"And those aliens might be sending the same signals too."

Her voice echoes beneath the observatory dome, slowly fading into silence as I think about what this means.

"So that's what you're doing?" I say. "Trying to tune in to alien TV? What are the chances that you'll find the right channel?"

Still looking at my revision work sheet, Professor Forster laughs out loud.

"What's so funny?" I ask.

On the top of the page I've written my name, JAMIE DRAKE, next to the title, EQUATIONS WORK SHEET, but I haven't started any of the sums. I don't know what she's laughing at.

"I thought you already had the answer written down here," Professor Forster replies. Using her pen, she circles two of the words at the top of the work sheet, cutting the "S" off the second.

DRAKE EQUATION

"An astronomer called Frank Drake came up with a sum to work out how many intelligent alien civilizations there might be in the Milky Way. We call this sum the 'Drake Equation.'"

Flipping the work sheet over, Professor Forster starts to write a really complicated equation on the blank page.

$$N = R^* \times f_p \times n_e \times f_l \times f_i \times f_c \times L$$

My brain starts hurting even before she finishes writing it out. There's a reason why me and equations don't get along. For a start, I don't even understand what any of these letters mean.

Ignoring the baffled expression on my face, Professor Forster starts to explain.

"It's really quite simple. The equation is trying to work out N, the number of alien civilizations that we might be able to receive signals from. To get the answer to this, Frank Drake came up with a list of things that would stop an alien species from ever getting the chance to transmit their own TV signals. These are all the letters on the other side of the equation. They stand for the numbers of stars being formed in our galaxy, how many of these stars will have planets, how many of these planets can support life, how many of these will develop *intelligent* life, et cetera, et cetera. By multiplying all these factors together, the Drake Equation spits out the answer to your question of how many alien TV stations we might be able to tune in to." She looks at me with a grin. "Now do you understand?"

Now, I reckon Professor Forster must have a brain the size of a small planet, but I still haven't got a clue what she's talking about.

"Sort of," I lie. "So how many aliens are out there, according to this equation?"

"Well, the thing with the Drake Equation is that we have to estimate a lot of the numbers," Professor Forster replies with a wave of her hand. "We don't know exactly how many planets there are in the Milky Way, or how many of these are in the habitable zone of their star—"

"You mean in the Goldilocks zone?"

"That's right," she says, looking kind of impressed. "In fact, apart from the number of stars being formed, the rest of the numbers we plug in to the equation are just intelligent guesses. So depending on who you ask, you get a different answer every time. Frank Drake reckoned there could be as many as ten thousand alien civilizations out there in the Milky Way."

"Wow," I say, my mind filling with images of aliens from all the science-fiction films and TV shows I've watched with my dad. "But if there are so many of them out there, then why haven't we heard from them yet?"

"Well, space is a very big place," Professor Forster says, an impish gleam returning to her gaze. "But who's to say we haven't already received a message from E.T.?"

I sit right up in my chair.

"What do you mean?"

"Since the 1960s, we've been using radio telescopes to scan the skies in search of alien transmissions," Professor Forster explains. "And in 1977 the Big Ear Observatory in the United States received an unusually strong radio signal from the direction of the constellation of Sagittarius. A seventy-two-second signal transmitted on a frequency that astronomers believe would be used by an alien civilization attempting to communicate with other planets."

My jaw drops as I take in this mind-blowing information. I thought my dad's mission was going to be the first to make contact with aliens. I didn't know that E.T. had already phoned. Why didn't they teach us this at school?

"What did the message say?"

"There was no information encoded in the signal," Professor Forster replies. "It was a single-tone modulation—like a beacon beamed from the depths of space. The simplest way for any alien civilization to say 'We're here.'"

The words echo in my head. *We're here.* Maybe Minty is right after all. Maybe aliens really do exist.

"So who sent the signal?" I ask eagerly.

"We just don't know," Professor Forster sighs, glancing up at the hole in the roof of the observatory. "That one seventy-two-second burst of radio waves is the only signal we've ever received. Since then countless radio telescopes have tried to detect the signal again, but all we've heard is silence. If this was an alien civilization calling, then they've hung up the phone."

My initial excitement crumples into disappointment. I thought we'd actually made contact with aliens, not just heard a random burst of static from an outer-space radio station.

"Don't worry," Professor Forster says, seeing the frustration on my face. "We're still listening and looking for signs of intelligent life. And we've got more than just radio telescopes to help us nowadays. As well as searching for radio signals, we've got telescopes scanning the sky for laser transmissions too. Our satellites now use lasers to transmit vast amounts of information across huge distances, so imagine what an alien civilization could do with this technology. Maybe next time the aliens won't just send a beacon signal—maybe they'll send us their Internet."

I glance up at the huge telescope that towers above the astronomer like a rocket on a launchpad, its view of the stars now completely covered by clouds.

"But how can you see anything with this?" I ask.

Professor Forster glances around suspiciously, as if checking that we're alone, and then beckons me forward with her finger.

"Can you keep a secret, Jamie?" she says, dropping her voice low, as if she's scared of being overheard.

Leaning forward, I quickly nod that I can.

"That's not the telescope I'm using to search for alien transmissions," she whispers with a waggle of her finger. "This observatory is just the base for a mobile Laser Optical Ground Station that is hooked up to the Hubble Space Telescope."

I remember the strange high-tech machine that I saw outside, the mysterious letters on its side now making perfect sense. L.O.G.S.—Laser Optical Ground Station. That techno-spider was talking to the stars.

"The raw data from the Hubble Space Telescope is downloaded via satellite to the ground station," Professor Forster explains, keeping her voice low. She gestures toward her laptop, the small blue light on the ★ **L.O.G.S.**

modem flashing away. "I then analyze the data, searching for signs of extraterrestrial intelligence. If there's an alien world out there that's beaming laser signals into space, then the Hubble telescope will find it."

"Wait a second," I say, suddenly remembering the one big problem with this. "The Hubble Space Telescope stopped working last year. I know because my dad was in charge of Mission Control when the ISS astronauts tried to get it back online, but nothing worked."

From behind her braids, Professor Forster's smile now looks rather mischievous.

"I'm afraid that might have been down to me. The telescope didn't exactly stop working—it just got a new owner."

"You hacked the Hubble telescope?"

Professor Forster pulls a pained face as if deciding exactly what to say.

" 'Hacked' is a bit of a loaded word," she finally replies. "The Hubble Space Telescope was in line to be retired, but I figured out a way to extend its mission to help search for alien life. When NASA wouldn't listen, I decided to take matters into my own hands."

"You hacked the Hubble telescope," I repeat, unable to believe what I'm hearing. "My dad said that that telescope cost ten billion pounds, and you've just taken it for a joyride to look for little green men."

A worried frown creeps across the astronomer's face.

"You won't tell anyone, will you?"

Now it's my turn to grin.

"Why would I?" I laugh. "It's a brilliant idea! Have you found anything yet?"

With a sigh of relief, Professor Forster shakes her head.

"No, not yet," she replies. "But the latest download from Hubble is arriving now. Maybe in all this new data coming through, we'll find someone trying to say hello." She turns back toward her laptop and then tuts and hops off her desk.

"What's the matter?" I ask.

"Minor technical difficulties," Professor Forster replies, moving toward the door. "I just need to make a quick check on the ground station system outside." She pauses in the doorway, turning back to fix me with a warning stare. "Don't touch anything while I'm gone."

I hold up my hands.

"Don't worry about me. I'm not the one who steals satellites."

Raising an eyebrow in my direction, Professor Forster disappears through the door, the sound of her footsteps echoing through the observatory as she descends the stairs. But as I shake my head in disbelief at what I've discovered here, I hear a beep from my cell phone.

Thinking this will be Mom checking up on me, I glance down at the home screen. But instead of a text, I see the low battery icon telling me that I've got only

5 percent charge left. It will take me a good twenty minutes to walk home, and if Mom can't get hold of me, she'll only start to worry, so I need to recharge this phone.

I look around, and my eyes fall on Professor Forster's laptop. On its screen I can see a stream of data scrolling down, the ★ L.O.G.S. modem plugged into the laptop still flashing away. But next to this, another USB cable dangles emptily. . . .

With a quick glance over my shoulder to check that the coast is clear, I plug the other end of this cable into my cell phone. A quick five-minute charge should give enough battery life to see me home. But as the USB connects, making the familiar three-note sound, I see a pop-up box suddenly appear on the laptop screen.

DATALINK CONNECTED
INCOMING TRANSMISSION FROM
HUBBLE SPACE TELESCOPE
DOWNLOADING TO DEVICE

Oh no. No, no, no. I don't want to connect my phone to the Hubble Space Telescope—I just want to recharge it. Leaning forward, I slide my finger across the laptop's touch pad, searching the screen for the cursor to close this window down. But before I can find it, I hear the sound of footsteps climbing back up the stairs.

Panicking, I make a grab for my phone, quickly yanking the USB cable out but in the process knocking over a nearby mug of tea. As the spilled liquid chugs across the desk, Professor Forster appears in the doorway.

"Just a glitch in the ground station feed," she announces. Then she sees me standing over her laptop, a pool of tea spreading from the upturned mug and dripping onto the floor. "What have you done?"

"I'm sorry," I say, grabbing hold of my revision work sheet to try and rescue it from the flood. "I just—"

Righting the mug, Professor Forster quickly pulls a handkerchief out of her cardigan pocket and begins to mop up the spill. On her tea-splattered laptop, a stream of data is still rolling down the screen as the ★ L.O.G.S. modem blinks on and off.

"This is supposed to be a working observatory," she snaps. "Not some after-school homework club. I think you'd better go, Jamie, before you cause any more damage."

Feeling my cheeks burn, I snatch up the rest of my stuff from the desk, and as Professor Forster wipes down her laptop, I make a run for the door.

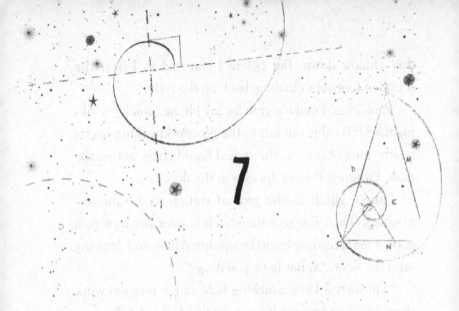

7

UP IN MY ROOM, I PICK MY WAY PAST THE SLOT-CAR RACE
track that covers most of the floor and flop down on my
bed. I feel absolutely stuffed. Luckily, turning up with
fish and chips for everyone stopped Mom from moaning
that I was a bit late when I got back from Beacon Hill,
although Granddad still grumbled that I hadn't got him a
pickled egg.

From downstairs I hear the sudden blare of the TV,
the volume turned to eleven so that Granddad can hear
the football commentary. I wrap my pillow around my
ears to try to block out the noise, but this hardly seems
to muffle the sound. I wish we had our own house. I can't

wait for Dad to get back so we can move out of Granddad's and find our own home again.

From across the landing, I hear Mom shout to Granddad to turn the TV down from eleven. There's no chance of getting Charlie to sleep with the Champions League on at full blast. As the roar of the crowd quiets slightly, I can't stop myself from thinking about how I made such a mess of things at the observatory.

It's funny, but just being there for that short time almost made me forget how much I was missing Dad. I felt closer to him somehow with all that talk about space and telescopes and stuff. It was like I was at Mission Control helping to keep him safe as he zoomed overhead in the International Space Station. Now there's no way Professor Forster's going to let me back in there, after I spilled tea all over her laptop.

As the fish and chips churn in my stomach, I stare at my Lego models on the shelf above my bed. Dad always brings me back a new set when he comes home from a trip away, and then we build it together. There's a Lego Big Ben, a Taj Mahal, the Eiffel Tower, Brandenburg Gate, and even the White House. It's like a Lego tour of the architectural wonders of the world, although most of my builds are only half-finished, as there's never enough time to complete them before Dad has to go away again. But when he gets back from the International Space Station,

Dad's *promised* me we'll get them all finished. He even says he's got me the best Lego set yet for my birthday. I can't wait to find out what it is.

Sitting up, I grab hold of the Lego catalog that's on my bedside table. I've already marked most of the pages with Post-it notes to give my mom some birthday present hints, but as I start to flick through my wish list, I hear a strange buzzing sound.

It's like a low hum, almost too faint to hear, that seems to be coming from somewhere close by. The roar of the crowd from the TV downstairs drowns it out for a second, but the attacking team must have lost the ball, because the crowd's roar turns to a disappointed groan.

I hear the buzzing sound again. I look out the window, thinking maybe that it's one of the planes from the nearby air force base, but the night sky is completely clear. Then I feel a vibration from my pocket and finally work out where the sound is coming from. It's my cell phone. I don't know why I didn't realize this before.

Puzzled, I pull the phone out of my pocket. Now, my cell isn't some top-of-the-line smartphone—it's an out-dated Motorola that used to belong to my dad before he got an upgrade. It can receive calls and send texts, but Mom disabled the roaming Internet. She says she doesn't want me running up an astronomical phone bill. The only apps that I've got are a calculator to help me with my math, a music player that's still filled with Dad's favorite tunes, and this ISS tracker app that lets me follow the International Space Station as it flies around the world. When I'm really missing Dad, I can just click on the app to find out exactly where he is.

I look at the screen. Nobody's calling me. There are no missed calls, no new texts or notifications, but I can feel the phone vibrating in my hand, the buzzing sound even louder now.

Then I see it. In the top-left corner of the home screen is a brand-new icon. It looks like a golden spiral, and as I stare at it, it seems to spin in time with the phone's vibration.

This is kind of weird. I don't remember downloading any new apps. How did this get on my phone?

Curious, I tap the spiral icon, eager to find out exactly what it is. As I touch the screen, I yelp in surprise as the tip of my finger suddenly glows with a golden light. A strange tingling sensation crawls over my skin like an electric shock in slow motion, but somehow without any pain. When I pull my finger away, the golden glow at the tip fades as quickly as it came. Goose bumps prickle my skin as I stare in disbelief at the disappearing glow.

The phone is quiet now, the buzzing silenced as the spiral on the screen still shimmers with a golden light. Nervous, I gently tap it again. But this time, nothing happens.

What *is* this weird app? The only thing I can think is it must be some kind of virus. Maybe I accidentally downloaded it when I plugged in my cell phone to Professor Forster's laptop. If she knows how to hack the Hubble Space Telescope, I wouldn't be surprised if there's something nasty lurking on her hard drive. But who ever heard of a computer virus that can turn your fingertip into a flashlight?

Before I can swipe on the spiral to try and find out more, I hear another roar from the TV downstairs, this one even louder than the last. As I brace myself for Mom to start shouting at Granddad again, the crowd's roar suddenly snaps into silence, followed by a crash and the sound of breaking glass.

Dropping my phone onto the bed, I race to the top of the stairs to find out what's going on. Mom and Charlie are already there, my little sister dressed in her Peppa Pig pajamas. Then from downstairs comes the sound of Granddad shouting a rather rude word.

"What's happening?" I ask as Mom clamps her hands over Charlie's ears.

Mom frowns.

"I think your granddad has thrown the TV out the window."

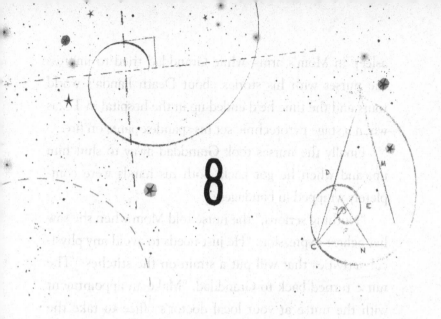

8

I CAN'T STOP MYSELF FROM YAWNING AS MRS. SOLOMON
hands out the math test papers.

It turned out Granddad hadn't thrown the TV out the window, but just tripped on the living room rug when he was trying to take a closer look at United's first goal. Falling forward, he'd grabbed hold of the TV to try and save himself but only managed to pull it off the wall. That was the sound of breaking glass that we'd heard, and the swearing was when Granddad landed in it, hands first.

So Mom, Charlie, and I ended up spending three hours in the ER last night, waiting for the doctors to sew Granddad's cuts. Charlie had spent most of the time curled up asleep in Mom's arms, while Granddad tried to impress the nurses with his stories about Death Panda's world tours and the time he'd ended up in the hospital in Texas when a stage pyrotechnic set his spandex pants on fire.

Finally the nurses took Granddad away to shut him up, and when he got back, both his hands were completely wrapped in bandages.

"Nothing serious," the nurse told Mom when she saw her aghast expression. "He just needs to avoid any physical activities that will put a strain on the stitches." The nurse turned back to Granddad. "Make an appointment with the nurse at your local doctor's office to take the stitches out in a week's time."

"What about playing my guitar?" Granddad protested.

"No guitar for a week," the nurse replied sternly. "You need to give your hands time to heal."

So even though I wasted most of Tuesday evening in a hospital waiting room, it wasn't all bad news. I only wish I'd remembered to take my equations work sheet with me so I could have studied for this test.

"Now, there's forty-five minutes until break, so try to answer every question," Mrs. Solomon says, walking back to the front of the classroom as next to me Minty mimes throwing up all over her test paper. "And remember, no calculators. It's important that you know how to balance these equations in your head. Don't forget, the Apollo 13 astronauts had to use mental arithmetic to work out the calculations they needed to get their damaged spacecraft back to Earth." Our teacher puts on her most serious expression. "You never know when an equation might save your life."

Feeling doubtful, I look down at the first question on the sheet in front of me.

Find the value of y. Show your work.
(a) 23 + y = 16 x 4

My heart sinks. I try to think back to what the revision sheet said about how to balance an equation, but all that really sticks in my head is what Professor Forster told me about the Drake Equation: how there could be ten thousand alien civilizations in our galaxy and we're just waiting for them to pick up the phone.

I've probably got more chance of a Martian calling me up on my cell than I have of finding out the value of y. I wish I could use a calculator.

At the front of the class, Mrs. Solomon is now sitting behind her desk, starting to mark a huge pile of exercise books as the rest of the class begin scribbling their answers. From where I'm sitting, I'm almost out of her sight.

This gives me an idea. Keeping one eye on my teacher, I slowly slide my cell phone out of my pocket. It might not get the Internet without any Wi-Fi, but at least it's got a calculator. I tap the screen to bring the phone to life.

The first thing I notice is that the weird spiral icon is now taking up half of the home screen. It's like it's grown overnight, the golden spiral spinning silently as my jaw drops in surprise. With Granddad's accident last night, I didn't have the chance to find out what this is. I click on the spiral to try and drag it out of the way. But with a low buzz of protest, the icon stays fixed to the screen. I touch the icon again, pressing hard and swiping, all at the same time, but no matter what I do, it just won't move at all.

There's a strange tingle in my finger, but I don't have time to worry about that now. I just have to concentrate on answering these test questions first. Tapping the apps list, I open up the calculator. If I want to find out the value of y, then I need to work out the other half of this equation. I tap in 16×4 and press the equals sign. The answer appears on the screen right away.

0

That's not right. I might not be that hot at mental arithmetic, but even I know that sixteen times four doesn't equal zero. I try to press clear, but the number just stays on the screen. Then another number appears next to it, followed by another and another—a whole string of numbers slowly filling the screen.

56

0 1 1 2 3 5 8 13 21 34 55 89 144 233 377
610 987 1597 2584 4181 6765 10946 17711
28657 46368 75025 121393 196418 317811
514229 832040 1346269

The numbers keep on coming, each one bigger than the last. And no matter which button I press, they won't go away. First that weird golden spiral thing and now this. My cell phone has officially lost it.

I jab my finger at the screen again, but the phone just buzzes angrily. Then I hear a pointed cough and look up to see Mrs. Solomon staring disapprovingly in my direction.

"Put it away, Jamie," she says, the tone of her voice now suddenly stern. "No calculators *or* cell phones are to be used in today's test."

Next to me, Minty snickers.

Feeling my face flush, I slip my cell phone back into my pocket. My stupid phone won't even let me cheat without giving me away. As Mrs. Solomon keeps her gaze fixed in my direction, I turn my attention back to the test paper.

But as I look again at the first question, something seems to click inside my brain. I feel a faint buzz behind my eyes, almost as if someone has flicked a switch on, and as I stare at the equation, I suddenly realize that I know the right answer.

$$y = 41$$

Quickly writing this down, I glance at the rest of the equations on the page. Moments before, I thought these looked impossible, but now each one makes perfect sense to me. I can't write the answers down quickly enough.

Turning the test sheet over, I take a look at the last question.

Now create your own equation.

Usually this type of question totally throws me, but now I don't even pause to think as the perfect equation pops into my head. It's so simple, I can't stop myself from smiling as I start to write the answer out.

$$-\tfrac{1}{2}\partial_\nu g_\mu^a\,\partial_\nu g_\mu^a - g_s f^{abc}\partial_\mu g_\nu^a g_\mu^b g_\nu^c - \tfrac{1}{4}g_s^2 f^{abc} f^{ade}\, g_\mu^b g_\nu^c g_\mu^d g_\nu^e +$$

As the bell rings for break, my pen jumps in surprise, leaving a trail of three dots at the end of the line. I feel like this test has only just started, but somehow it's break time already. I shake my head. It feels like I'm waking from a dream.

For the first time, I notice that Minty is staring at me in disbelief. Then I look down at our desk, my side of it covered with half a dozen pieces of paper, some spilling off the edge and falling onto the floor. I don't know where they've come from, but every page is filled with hundreds of letters, symbols, and numbers. A second ago everything seemed so clear, but now, as I stare down at the scribbled pages, they don't seem to make any sense at all.

"Okay," Mrs. Solomon says, looking up as she closes the last of the exercise books on her desk. "Hand in your test papers to me, and I'll see you after break for your next Space Week challenge."

Confused, I quickly gather up the scattered pages before Mrs. Solomon notices them. Shoving these into my bag, I just keep hold of the topmost sheet, handing this in to my teacher as I head for the door.

"Well done, Jamie," Mrs. Solomon says as she glances down at the test paper, her features creased in an encouraging smile. "It was good to see you trying so hard at the end. You see, you don't need a cell phone to help you with your math, do you?"

I shake my head, trying to ignore the new buzzing vibration from the depths of my pocket. Whatever just happened, I feel certain it's got something to do with the weird new icon on my phone.

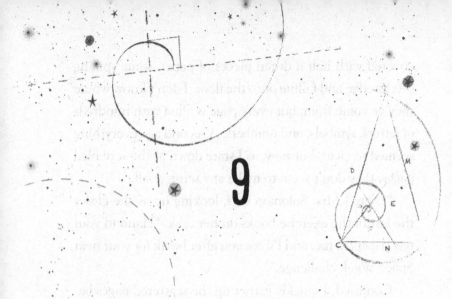

9

I SIT ON THE LOW BRICK WALL, STARING AT MY CELL PHONE. On the playground, most of the boys in my class are staging a soccer rerun of last night's Champions League match. Usually I'd be right there in the middle of the action, but I can't stop watching this spinning spiral in the center of the home screen. It looks even larger than before, its golden curve growing wider as the spiral unwinds. I think it's trying to take over my phone.

My dad says that when something goes wrong in space, you need to "work the problem." This means breaking a situation down step-by-step in order to find the right answer. Astronauts need to think about all the possibilities to help them identify the correct solution. It could mean the difference between life and death.

If I want to find out what this weird spiral is, that's what I need to do now. I've got to work the problem.

First step is to think about when it first showed up on my phone. It was only after I got back from the observatory that the buzzing started. This must mean I downloaded it when I connected my cell to Professor Forster's laptop.

The next step is to think about what it is. The most logical answer is some kind of computer virus. This fits with some of the weird stuff my phone has been doing—the annoying buzzing sound, the way my calculator went screwy and started spitting out all those random numbers. A computer virus could do all those things, right?

But then I think about the other strange things that have been happening. The way my fingertip lit up like a flashlight when I touched the spiral for the first time. And then how time seemed to disappear during that math test. One minute I'm writing out my own equation, the next the bell is ringing for break and my desk is covered with scrawled pieces of paper, every page filled with letters and numbers that look more like Egyptian hieroglyphics.

In my head, I can picture the pop-up message that appeared on Professor Forster's laptop when I plugged in my phone. It said there was an incoming transmission from the Hubble Space Telescope. . . .

On the screen the golden spiral is still spinning, the phone silently vibrating in my hand. A thrilling thought jumps to the front of my brain. What if I downloaded this from outer space?

Professor Forster said she was using the Hubble telescope to search for signs of extraterrestrial life. What if this spiral is the signal she's searching for?

The shape of a girl-size shadow falls across me to interrupt this wild train of thought.

"How come you were acting so weird in class?" Minty says as I look up to see her silhouetted in the sun. "One second you're trying to cheat, and then the next it looked like you were writing out the longest sum in the world."

I don't know what to say, so I just shrug.

Minty sits down on the wall next to me.

As if annoyed by Minty's presence, my cell phone gives an angry buzz.

"Text from your dad?" Minty asks.

I glance down at my phone. In the center of the screen, the golden spiral is slowly revolving.

I shake my head.

"It's just this stupid phone," I say, showing Minty my cell. "It keeps on buzzing for no reason at all."

"No wonder," Minty laughs. "I mean, your phone is seriously ancient."

"It's not that," I reply, bristling slightly. "It's just—"

A soccer ball thuds into the wall next to us, missing Minty's legs by a centimeter or two.

"Hey!" she shouts out angrily. "Do I look like a goal-post?"

Then, with a flick of her hair, Minty turns her attention back to me.

"Do you miss him?"

"Who?" I say, slightly distracted by a strange tingling sensation in my fingers.

"Your dad."

Stuffing the phone in my pocket to try and escape its vibrations, I nod in reply.

"Yeah, of course I do. I mean, I get to chat to him most nights, and I can see him on TV and stuff, but it's not the same as having him here."

Minty sniffs.

"I know," she says. "It's the same for me."

Puzzled, I shoot Minty a questioning look.

"What do you mean? When was your dad on TV?"

"He was on *Crimewatch*," Minty replies. "Although it wasn't really him."

My dad's an astronaut. Minty's is a bank robber. Space hero. Career criminal. It's not the same at all. I'm just trying to think of the best way to tell her this when Minty asks me another question.

"When's your dad coming home?"

"He lands back on Earth in nine days," I say. "Then he'll have a ton of medical tests and press conferences to do, but I hope he'll be home pretty soon after that."

Minty sniffs again.

"My dad doesn't get out for another ten years. I might have left home by the time he comes home."

The soccer ball thuds against the wall again, but this time Minty doesn't say a thing.

I imagine Dad being stuck in space for another ten years. On the ISS, he travels all the way around the world every ninety-two minutes. One minute he's over Great Britain, the next he's racing across the Atlantic Ocean. When we speak on the phone, Dad sometimes tells me what he can see through the cupola window: deserts and lakes, cities and mountains, the landscape changing constantly as day turns to night and back again in the space of an hour. He makes it all sound so amazing, but the only sight I really want to see is Dad.

And Minty has to wait ten years for hers. . . .

I don't know what to say, so I decide to change the subject.

"Minty, do you really believe in aliens?"

"Uh-huh." Minty sniffs, wiping her face with the sleeve of her dress. "The evidence is inarguable."

"And do you think they might be sending us messages?"

"All the time," Minty replies.

I feel the phone vibrate in my pocket, the strange tingling now creeping up the back of my neck.

"And these messages," I say, raising my voice as the buzzing sound from my pocket grows louder. "Do you think the aliens could send them to a cell phone?"

Minty laughs out loud.

"Don't be stupid," she says. "The roaming charges would be massive."

The school bell rings across the playground.

"Come on," Minty says, jumping to her feet. "Let's find out what our next stupid space challenge is."

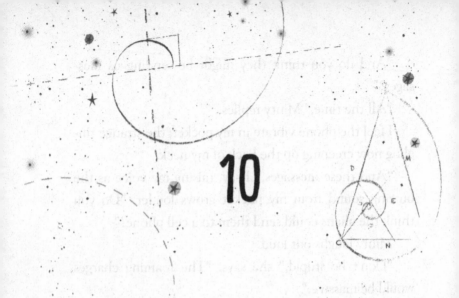

"CAN YOU IMAGINE AN ALIEN WORLD?"

Mrs. Solomon gestures toward the posters she's stuck up around the walls of our classroom. They show scenes from some of my favorite science-fiction films. There's Luke Skywalker riding a tauntaun across the icy wastes of Hoth, its gray-white fur almost lost in the snowy landscape. I can see the lush jungle moon of Pandora with its floating mountains and forests teeming with alien life. There's Superman's dad standing alone as Krypton burns. It's like Class Six is the sun at the center of a science-fiction solar system.

"All these alien worlds have been imagined by artists

and directors," our teacher says, pointing to each picture in turn. "Cloud cities and mechanical planets, crystal mountains and desert moons. Now I want you to use your artistic skills to create your own alien worlds."

On the desk in front of me is a large sheet of poster board. Jars of colored pencils, pastels, wax crayons, and charcoal mark the border of Minty's half of the desk. She got first dibs on all the best felt-tips and is already starting to draw the outline of some wild alien scene.

Minty's the best artist in our class. In fact, she's probably the best artist in the whole school. She does these brilliant cartoons in the school newspaper, and when Mrs. Solomon wanted some scenery for our class musical of *Macbeth*, Minty helped paint this really spooky castle with headless ghosts and skeletons everywhere. When we did the play, our advisor, Mr. Hayes, even had to cover up some bits of scenery because the first graders found them too scary. I bet the alien world she creates is going to look amazing.

Mrs. Solomon floats around the class in her flowery dress, throwing out her usual words of encouragement.

"Beautiful yellows and greens, Jasmine."

"Amazing patterns, Lila."

"Lovely bold lines, Aaron. Are those tentacles?"

I look back down at my blank sheet of paper. I don't have a clue what to draw.

"Are you stuck?" Minty asks, chewing on her pen lid as she looks up from her cartoon of an intergalactic scrapyard. In this, a huge metal dinosaur is munching on a pile of rusting robots, the jet-black sky filled with a Death Star moon. "If you can't think of anything, then just draw an ice world. They're simple—the only color you need is white."

I shake my head, my mind as blank as my piece of paper. I don't think Mrs. Solomon would be very impressed with an invisible planet. But before Minty can offer another suggestion, an insistent buzz sounds from my pants pocket.

"Is that somebody's cell phone?" Mrs. Solomon inquires, irritation flashing across her features. "Remember the school rules, please. If you don't turn it off right away, it's getting confiscated."

She glances around to find the culprit. Digging deep in my pocket, I clamp my hand around the phone to mute the buzzing sound. As my fingers close around its metal case, I feel a strange vibration, right behind my eyes. I blink—the buzzing of my phone instantly replaced by a silence that seems to make time stand still.

"Have you finished, Jamie?"

I open my eyes to see Mrs. Solomon now standing over my desk, her face creased in admiration. For a second, I feel totally confused. How did she get from there to here so quickly? Then I look down at my desk, my blank sheet of paper now filled with the most incredible picture.

Twin suns shine in a bright purple sky above a vast forest of giant plants and ferns. Black flowers bloom in every direction, and rising above these, huge golden spirals shimmer like trapped sunlight. The shape of these unearthly skyscrapers is the same as the spiral icon on my phone, but as I stare in wonder at this impossible picture, I see that each golden spiral is actually a sprawling alien city winding into the sky.

"This is amazing," Mrs. Solomon says, peering intently at the poster that covers my desk. "How did you capture such incredible detail with oil pastels?"

I look down at my hands. My fingers are smeared with purple, green, and gold, a rainbow of pastels scattered across my desk. In the picture, the colors almost seem to be alive—like this alien landscape is just frozen in time.

Did I really draw this?

When I closed my eyes, this page was blank and then, when I opened them a split second later, this amazing world was here. I must be going mad.

"What an imagination," my teacher murmurs as Minty stares at my picture openmouthed.

But as I rack my brain trying to work out what's happening to me, the only thing I know for sure is that the mind that imagined this picture isn't mine. So whose mind is it?

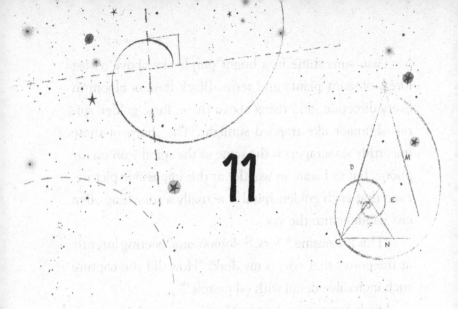

11

THE FIRST THING I WANT TO DO WHEN I GET HOME FROM school is head straight for the observatory at the top of Beacon Hill. I've got to find Professor Forster and tell her what's happening to me. If this golden spiral on my phone is some kind of alien message that I've downloaded from the Hubble Space Telescope, then she'll know what to do.

But when I open the back door, I see Hayley sitting at the kitchen table with Granddad, and I remember that it's time for our weekly video conference with Dad. Hayley Collins was the first British astronaut to walk in outer space. Ten years ago she was on the International Space

Station, just like Dad is now. She took part in a two-person EVA—that's an extravehicular activity, or space walk for short—to repair a solar panel that had been damaged by a micrometeorite strike.

Hayley is our family escort. This means that while Dad's in space she's the person who helps to look after Mom, Charlie, and me—keeping us up to speed with everything that's happening with Dad's mission. Hayley makes sure that all our communications with the ISS—like our weekly family video conference—run smoothly. If there's any problem that needs sorting, she's the person who can call Mission Control and put us straight through to Dad.

Sometimes it can get a bit scary, worrying about all the things that could go wrong while Dad's up there in space, but Hayley's always great at keeping us calm. One of the first times we talked to Dad on the ISS via video link, Charlie suddenly started shrieking as the face of a giant ant filled the screen. It was really a normal-size ant that had escaped from one of the experiments on board the space station—it just looked huge as it floated in front of the camera lens. Dad had to quickly abort the video call so he could capture the ant, but when the screen went black, Charlie just kept on screaming. She was convinced that the International Space Station had been invaded by giant alien bugs and that Dad was going to be eaten alive. Mom and I tried to explain about the ant experiment, but Charlie wouldn't listen. Only Hayley could get her to calm down by saying that the ISS had a Space Bug Zapper installed that splatted any alien invaders as soon as they appeared. Charlie stopped crying then, and when Dad reappeared on the screen ten minutes later, my little sister just wanted him to show her all the zapped aliens. Me and Mom had been too busy trying to make Charlie understand, while Hayley just focused on stopping my sister from worrying. Hayley says that's what astronauts do—solve the problem in front of them.

"Hi, Jamie," Hayley says, putting down her mug of tea to greet me with a smile. "Ready to talk to your dad?"

This is our last family video call before Dad's space walk. When he comes home next week, we won't need a "family escort" anymore. I think I'm going to miss her.

"Is this the last time you're coming to see us?" I ask.

"No, silly." Hayley grins. "I'll be back on Friday for your dad's space walk. We'll watch the Light Swarm launch together—Mission Control has arranged for a live link with your dad's helmet cam. You'll get to see an astronaut's view of the EVA." She can't hide her excitement. "I wouldn't miss it for the world."

At the mention of Dad's space walk, my stomach does a somersault. For a second, I think I'm just nervous about Dad's mission, but then it gurgles again. I really need to go to the toilet.

"Well, if you're all off to speak to Dan Dare," Granddad says, getting up from the table with a groan, "I'm going out to the barn to give my drum kit a good thrashing. That blinking nurse didn't say anything about me not playing the drums."

So while Granddad heads to the barn to vent his frustration and Hayley phones Mission Control, I make a dash for the bathroom.

I'm just zipping my pants back up when I hear a buzzing sound above the noise of the toilet flushing.

I pull my cell phone out of my pocket. In the center of the home screen, the golden spiral is still spinning, the icon looking even larger than it did last time. The phone vibrates again in the palm of my hand. I feel the same tingling sensation that I felt behind my eyes just before things got strange at school.

I still don't know how that weird alien picture got onto my sheet of paper. I don't remember drawing anything at all. And even if I did, there's no way I could have made an amazing picture like that. I usually can't even draw stickmen without making a mistake, but that extraterrestrial landscape almost looked like a photograph.

My finger hovers over the golden spiral, wishing I could just click to unlock this mystery.

"What are you?" I murmur, trying to make sense of it all. The cell phone vibrates again, sending a strange tingle up my arm. As the toilet flush finally gurgles into silence, all I can hear is a constant hum that seems to be coming from my phone. Then through the drone, I hear a voice crackling from the speaker.

"We are—BZZZ. We are—BZZZZ."

I stare at my phone openmouthed.

"Hello?" I say, holding the phone close to my ear. "Who's there?"

There's no reply. My cell phone has stopped vibrating, and the only buzzing is coming from a wasp that's just flown in through the bathroom window. Maybe I just imagined that voice. . . .

"We are the—BZZZZZ."

I nearly drop the phone down the toilet.

"Who are you?"

I'm so shocked that I can't stop myself from blurting out the answer.

"I'm—I'm Jamie," I stutter.

"Help BZZZ."

The voice coming from the speaker doesn't sound like a person. It's more robotic—like one of those phone calls you get when someone sends a text message to your home phone instead of your mobile. If this is a message from outer space, then maybe "Buzz" here is leaving a voice mail. . . .

74

But before I can listen to the rest of it, the bathroom door handle rattles, followed by the sound of Charlie's voice outside.

"Jamie, come quick!" she squeals. "Daddy's on TV!"

"I'll be right there," I shout.

Switching my phone into silent mode, I quickly shove it back into my pocket. If I've really downloaded some kind of intergalactic distress signal, then my spaceman dad will know what to do.

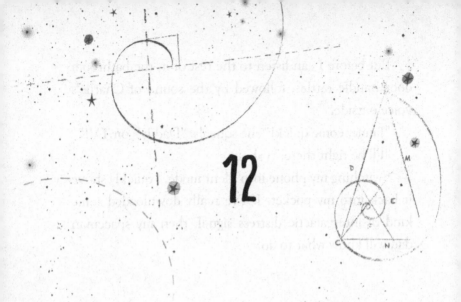

12

SQUEEZED NEXT TO MOM AND CHARLIE ON THE SOFA, I STARE
at Dad's face on our brand-new TV—this one fixed higher
up on the wall so Granddad can't pull it down. Behind
Dad I can see a tangle of wires and cables snaking around
the interior of the International Space Station. Back here
on Earth, Hayley is sitting in the armchair next to the living room door, out of sight of the video camera but still
close by in case anything goes wrong with the connection.

"Hey, guys," Dad says, his face breaking into a smile.
"How are you doing?"

Because of the satellite relay, there's always a two-
second delay between the moment Dad speaks and when

we hear him. At first this made our video calls a bit of a nightmare, as Charlie kept getting upset when Dad didn't seem to be listening to her right away, but we've worked out a system now. Charlie talks first so she can tell Dad her news, while Mom and me wait for our turn.

So while Charlie starts telling Dad about how she fed the bunnies at nursery school today, I think about what just happened with my phone.

Professor Forster said that the only extraterrestrial signal the human race has ever received was a seventy-two-second beacon beamed from the stars. On Friday, Dad's sending a swarm of space probes to Tau Ceti—one of our nearest stars—but they'll still take fifteen years to get there, traveling near light speed. And any information they beam back will take another fifteen years to reach Earth. So if Buzz is a message sent from some alien planet, how come it's talking back to me?

On the rug in front of the TV, Charlie's showing Dad how she's learned to do a cartwheel. Collapsing in a giggling heap on the floor, she squeals with delight as Dad demonstrates a space somersault, his head disappearing backward as his knees and legs fill the screen before flipping right around again.

"Again! Again!" Charlie squeals, still giggling uncontrollably. Then she stops and turns toward Mom with a worried look on her face. "I think I've done a pee."

"Never mind," Mom replies with a weary sigh. Getting up from the sofa, she takes Charlie by the hand.

"I'll just have to get her a change of clothes, Dan," Mom says as Dad raises a guilty hand in apology. "Why don't you have a chat with Jamie?"

On the TV screen, I watch as Dad plucks a floating pen out of the air.

"Oops, pen overboard," he says. "One of the hazards of space gymnastics." He tucks this back into his top pocket and then nods as if hearing Mom's reply. "So how are things with you, son?"

I don't know what to say. From the hallway, I can still hear Charlie complaining as Mom leads her up the stairs. The silence lengthens to six, seven, eight seconds—my brain still trying to find the right words.

"Are you still receiving me?" Dad asks, leaning toward the camera with a frown.

"We're still receiving you, Dan," Hayley calls out brightly from the other side of the room. "Jamie's just having a bit of a think."

She gets up out of her chair. "I'll just go and give your mom a hand with Charlie," she says, moving toward the door. "Give you and your dad some space to talk."

"Is everything okay?" Dad asks, his voice overlapping with the end of Hayley's sentence as she heads out of the room.

I watch him bob in microgravity, his face still creased in concern.

"Dad," I say, "I think I've got aliens on my phone."

There's a pause as my words zoom four hundred kilometers up into space. Then Dad laughs out loud.

"Good one, Jamie," he says with a grin. "Is this some new game you've got, then? I thought Mom wasn't too keen on you downloading things to your phone."

"No, Dad." I try to explain, struggling to put it all into words. "I think it's a real alien message. You see, I downloaded it from the Hubble Space Telescope. At first I thought it was some kind of computer virus, as it just kept on buzzing all the time, but then it tried to turn my finger into a flashlight. All these really weird things have been happening at school today, and now it's started talking to me. It says its name is Buzz. I think it's—"

"Whoa," Dad says, the echo of his voice cutting across mine. "Slow down, Jamie—you're not making any sense."

I pause to catch my breath. It's weird. Dad might be the one who's weightless, but I kind of feel lighter too, now that I've told him everything.

Dad has always said I can tell him anything—any problem I've got, any worry I have, and he'll help me to sort it out. That's why it's been so hard with him up in space, especially when the main thing I'm worried about is him being up in space. Now at least I've got my own

79

problem for him to sort out. All I need is for Dad to believe me and then he'll be able to tell me what to do.

"First of all, the Hubble Space Telescope stopped working last year," Dad says. "So you couldn't have downloaded anything from it—especially not an alien message."

"I know, but Professor Forster hacked into the telescope."

"Who's Professor Forster?"

"She's an astronomer," I tell him. "I met her at the observatory at the top of Beacon Hill. She's looking for aliens, just like you."

"Jamie, my mission's a bit more complicated than that—"

"I think the signal might be some kind of distress call. Buzz says they need help—"

Our sentences are overlapping now, the satellite delay causing our words to crash into each other. Raising his hand, Dad waits until there's a moment of silence, and then he starts to speak again.

"I know this mission has been hard on you, Jamie," he says. "Especially with me missing your birthday on Friday. But you don't have to make up this story about alien messages just to get my attention."

"It's not a story," I protest, pulling out my cell phone. On the home screen the golden spiral is frozen midspin. Taking the phone out of silent mode, I tap my finger against the screen, but nothing happens. No buzzing sound. No robotic voice. Nothing to prove that I'm telling the truth.

"It is true," I say, holding the phone up to the camera so Dad can see the home screen. "I think this spiral is the alien signal. I just need you to help me work out what it means. . . ."

On the TV screen, Dad's frown deepens as he listens to my words.

That's when I realize. He doesn't believe me.

My voice trails into silence. I don't know what else I can say.

"Look, Jamie," Dad replies, his face still creased in concern. "After Friday, the Lux Aeterna mission will be complete. The Light Swarm probes will be on their way to Tau Ceti, and I can head for home. Why don't you show me this 'signal' when I get back and we can work out what it is then?"

Dad's mission is all about searching for signs of alien life, so why won't he believe what I'm saying? But before I can say anything else, Mom walks back into the living room.

"Hayley's helping Charlie get dressed," she announces as she sits back down on the sofa. "She wants to show you the space suit costume she's going to wear to school after your space walk on Friday."

While she waits for Dad to get the message via the satellite relay, Mom turns toward me.

"Could I just have a word with your dad on my own for a bit, Jamie?" she asks. "We've got a few things we need to discuss in private."

Still feeling let down by Dad's reaction, I nod.

"I've got to go now, Dad," I say, getting up from the sofa. "I'll see you soon."

"Bye, Jamie," Dad calls out, holding up his hand like he always does. "And have a great birthday on Friday. I'll be thinking of you, son."

I press my hand against his on the TV screen, trying my hardest not to cry. I wish he were home right now so I could talk to him properly.

It's strange, but as I close the door behind me, there's only silence. It's as though Mom's waiting until the coast is clear until she talks to Dad. It's not really fair that she's hijacked our family video call just to have a private chat with Dad. What's so private that they can't talk about it in front of me anyway? And then the answer jumps into my head—my birthday present.

Dad said he got me the best Lego set yet, but how's he going to get it to me from up there in space? Standing completely still, I press my ear to the door. If I'm going to have a birthday surprise on Friday, I want to find out what it is.

For a second, I still can't hear a thing. Then the sound of Mom's voice comes through the door.

"I got the letter from your attorney, Dan."

There's another two seconds of silence and then I hear Dad's reply.

"Well, we both agreed it was for the best. I thought it would help to get things moving."

Mom laughs, but from where I'm standing behind the door, this doesn't sound like a happy laugh. I'm starting to feel confused. What's this got to do with my birthday present?

"You've always got to be first, haven't you?" she says. "Even when it comes to getting an attorney."

I still don't know what they're talking about. Being an astronaut is a dangerous job. There are tons of things that can go wrong in space, and Dad says you've always got to be prepared for the worst. Maybe this letter from an attorney is to do with Dad's will—making sure that Mom, Charlie, and me are taken care of if anything goes wrong. Not that it will. He'll be back home safe next week.

But it's what I hear Dad say next that rips the ground from beneath my feet and sends my head spinning.

"Sixteen years of marriage is a long time, Ally. Long enough to work out that we both want different things. Let's try and keep this divorce civilized, like we both agreed."

I stand there completely frozen, my ear still glued to the door. I can't have heard this right. Mom and Dad love each other. How can they be getting divorced?

"When do you want to tell Jamie and Charlie?" Mom asks.

There's another long pause. Two seconds that feel like a lifetime to me.

"When I get back home," Dad says. "We'll tell them together."

Behind me, I hear the sound of my little sister stomping down the stairs.

"Look, Jamie!" Charlie yells. I turn to see a mini-astronaut standing at the bottom of the stairs. Charlie is dressed head to toe in a white jumpsuit with silver gloves and a big rocket badge. Her excited face beams out from her shiny space helmet. "I'm an astronaut!"

Behind her, Hayley peers at me with a puzzled look on her face.

"Are you okay, Jamie?" she asks. "Has your dad had to end the video call?"

"No," I say, quickly turning away. "Mom's still talking to him. I just need to get some fresh air."

As Charlie rushes into the living room to show Dad her space suit, I head for the kitchen. I open the door and step out into the backyard, staring through my tears up into a sky full of stars.

From the open barn door comes the thunderous sound of drums, Granddad's snare hits, and cymbal crashes, tracking the confusion that's now swirling around my head. Nothing makes any sense. I thought Mom and Dad were getting along better now. They haven't argued since Dad went into space. I thought they still loved each other. How can they be splitting up?

Ninety degrees above the horizon I see what looks like a bright star moving quickly across the sky. Automatically, I reach for the phone in my pocket, ready to check whether it's Dad passing overhead on the ISS. But on the home screen I see the golden spiral, still frozen midspin, and I remember that I've got something else to worry about.

And if Dad doesn't believe me, I know someone who will.

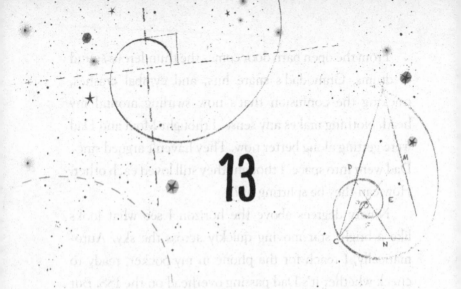

13

"SHOW ME," PROFESSOR FORSTER SAYS, LEANING FORWARD in her chair.

Above her head, the opening in the observatory dome is now closed, the huge telescope looking up only to see a rectangle of rust.

Kind of nervous, I pick up my cell phone. On the home screen, the golden spiral is still stationary, the phone completely silent. When I tried to prove to Dad that I was telling the truth, Buzz kept quiet. I tap my finger against the spiral icon, hoping that the tip of my finger will start glowing with a golden light. Nothing happens.

Determined not to give up, I hold the phone in front

of my mouth, the same way Captain Kirk uses his communicator in the *Star Trek* films.

"Buzz, are you receiving me?" I ask, my voice echoing around the deserted observatory. "It's me—Jamie Drake."

There's no reply.

Looking up, I see that Professor Forster's lips are pursed in a smile. She's trying her hardest not to laugh. I feel a sudden surge of anger welling up from deep inside.

"I'm telling the truth," I snap. "There's an alien signal on my phone. I've heard it speaking to me."

The astronomer shakes her head.

"Jamie, even if you have accidentally downloaded an alien transmission from the Hubble Space Telescope, there's no way you'd be able to understand it. We don't know what language an extraterrestrial civilization might use, but it certainly wouldn't be English."

I try and fight down the frustration that's boiling up inside me. Professor Forster doesn't believe me—just like Dad.

Lowering my gaze, I glare at the spiral on the phone's screen. Everything started going weird the moment this appeared: the strange voice buzzing from my phone, that alien picture that appeared on my desk out of nowhere, even those equations that I solved without a second thought. That's when I remember something else.

Tapping the apps list, I quickly open up the calculator.

"It's not just the voice," I explain. "When I was doing my math test, I tried to use my calculator app to work out a sum. But instead of giving me the right answer, my phone just started spitting out all these random numbers instead." The list of numbers is still frozen on the calculator screen. "But what if they're not random? What if they're coordinates showing where the signal was sent from?"

With a doubtful frown, Professor Forster takes the phone as I thrust it into her hand. But as she looks down at the numbers on the screen, her expression changes to one of disbelief.

"Am I right?" I ask excitedly. "Are they coordinates? Is this Buzz's address in outer space?"

Professor Forster shakes her head.

"These aren't coordinates," she says. "This is the Fibonacci sequence."

"The Fibber-what?"

"The Fibonacci sequence is a number pattern where each number in the sequence is the sum of the previous two."

Placing the phone on the table between us, Professor Forster points to the topmost line of numbers.

0 1 1 2 3 5 8 13 21 34 55 89 144 233 377 610 987

"Zero plus one equals one. One plus one equals two. One plus two equals three. Two plus three equals five. You can see as you add the previous two numbers, this gives you the next number in the sequence." She points farther along the line. "Fifty-five plus eighty-nine equals one hundred and forty-four. Eighty-nine plus one hundred and forty-four equals two hundred and thirty-three. One hundred and forty-four plus two hundred and thirty-three equals three hundred and seventy-seven."

She looks up at me, her eyes shining with excitement.

"This is not some random list of numbers, Jamie. We see the Fibonacci sequence all around us in the universe. The number of petals on a flower follows this pattern, as do the way branches grow on a tree. Generations of honeybees in a hive, the patterns on a pinecone, even the proportions of the human body match the Fibonacci numbers in strange and fascinating ways." Professor Forster grabs hold of a pen and starts to draw a series of connecting squares on the paper in front of her, each one growing larger than the last. "I can even show this pattern visually. If I use the Fibonacci numbers for the dimensions of these squares, I can then draw a line that joins them together."

She uses her pen to trace a line from the center of the page. As I watch the curving line spiral around, connecting the corners of each square in turn, the picture fits with a click in my mind.

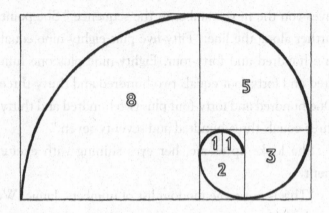

"This is called the Fibonacci spiral," Professor Forster explains, "and this precise form can be found in the shapes of seashells, hurricanes, even spiral galaxies."

As she lifts her pen from the page, the astronomer stares at the spiral she's just drawn. With a flicker of recognition, she starts to reach for my cell phone, but I've already snatched up the phone from the table, swiping back from the calculator app to reveal the golden spiral on the screen. My eyes flick between this and Professor Forster's drawing. The two spirals are exactly the same.

"Do you know what this means?" Professor Forster breathes. "Many scientists believe that if an alien civilization wanted to communicate with us they would choose a universal language that we share. Whatever planet we live on, we can all look up at the sky and count the stars. One plus one equals two, everywhere. Math might be the language that aliens use to 'talk' to us—sending this Fibonacci sequence could be their way of letting us know that the signal has been sent by an intelligent species."

"You mean you believe me?" I ask, unable to tear my eyes from the golden glow of the Fibonacci spiral on my phone. "You really think that Buzz is real?"

"I'm not saying that you've spoken to an alien," Professor Forster replies, holding up a cautionary hand. "The vast distances between Earth and even the nearest stars outside of the solar system mean that any kind of instant communication would be impossible. We can't have a cozy chat with E.T. on the phone if he's fifty light-years away. But if this signal is of extraterrestrial origin, the implications for the human race are profound. This would be the first proof that we are not alone in the universe."

"So what do we do?" I ask, barely able to hide my excitement.

Professor Forster holds out her hand for my phone.

"We bust open your cell phone and take a look inside. If this signal has been downloaded onto your SD card, I need to investigate this."

I jump in surprise as the phone begins to vibrate in my hand. Glancing down, I expect to see the spiral spinning in time with this insistent buzzing sound. But the golden icon is still frozen, stuck motionless on the screen. Instead I see a new text message notification—a painful reminder that aliens aren't my only problem.

Where are you? Mom X

It's time for me to go.

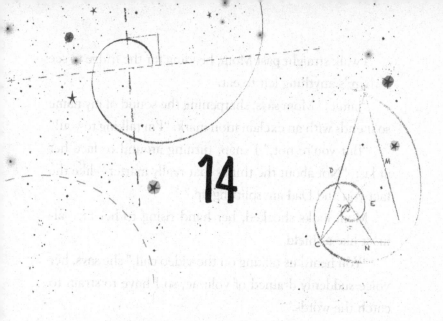

14

WHEN I GET BACK, MOM'S WAITING FOR ME AT THE KITCHEN table.

"Where did you disappear to?" she asks, the sharp tone in her voice telling me I'm in trouble. "I've been worried sick. I sent you a text half an hour ago but didn't get any reply. What's the point of you having a phone if I can't get hold of you?"

I don't say anything, just push my phone down deeper into my pocket, out of sight. Professor Forster wanted to keep hold of it to find out more about Buzz, but I raced from the observatory before she could take it. It's *my* phone.

I walk straight past Mom, heading for the fridge to see if there's anything left to eat.

"Jamie!" Mom says, sharpening the sound of my name so it ends with an exclamation mark. "I'm talking to you!"

"But you're not," I snap, turning around to face her at last. "Not about the things that really matter—like the fact you and Dad are splitting up."

Mom looks shocked, her hand rising to her face almost like a shield.

"You heard us talking on the video call," she says, her voice suddenly drained of volume, so I have to strain to catch the words.

I nod, trying to fight back my tears.

"Oh, Jamie," Mom says, getting up from her chair and reaching out to give me a hug. "I didn't want you to find out this way. Your dad and I wanted to tell you together."

I don't want a hug. I just want answers.

"What does it matter how I found out?" I explode. "You're still getting divorced!"

"Jamie, don't shout," Mom says, trying to keep her voice calm. "Your granddad's upstairs giving Charlie a bath. I don't want you upsetting your sister."

I think about my little sister and how she's going to feel when she finds out the truth about Mom and Dad. A horrible thought creeps into my head.

"What's going to happen to us?" I ask, wiping my eyes

with the edge of my sleeve. "Who are Charlie and me going to live with?"

"Well, these things are all to be properly decided," Mom says. "But your dad and I both think it makes most sense for you and Charlie to stay here with me at Grand-dad's."

I feel like I've just been punched in the stomach.

"But Dad's coming home next week," I protest. "Where's he going to stay?"

"Your dad's going to have to follow an intensive re-habilitation program to get him used to life back here on Earth," Mom explains. "For the first month, he'll be living in special quarters on the air force base. It's just half an hour's drive from here."

I think about all the different air force bases we've lived on as a family—never staying in one place long enough for me to make real friends. Dad's training trips taking him halfway around the world, away for weeks at a time. As I try to make sense of what's happening to us, all I can see inside my head are pictures of Dad saying goodbye.

It was my job to keep an eye on the Drake family solar system and make sure that everything kept spinning safely until Dad got home. What did I miss?

"Your dad still loves you, Jamie," Mom tells me, tak-ing my hands in hers. I can feel her fingers trembling, her empty words hanging in the air between us. "We both do. You know that, don't you?"

I shake my head, tears stinging my eyes again.

"I don't care," I say, snatching my hands away. "I just wanted you to tell me the truth."

Slamming the door behind me, I race up the stairs two at a time. I need to get inside my room before I start falling apart.

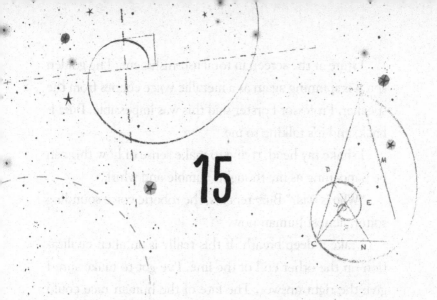

15

ON THE HOME SCREEN OF MY PHONE, THE GOLDEN SPIRAL IS
still frozen midspin, and I'm starting to wonder if Buzz
will ever speak again. I've got so many questions racing
around my head, but the one I really want to know the
answer to is the impossible one to ask. The only question
that might explain why my family is falling apart. I can
barely even whisper this to myself as I sit here alone in the
darkness of my room.

"Why doesn't Dad love us anymore?"

As if in answer to my question, the phone suddenly
vibrates.

"Who is Dad?"

I stare at the screen in total astonishment. The golden spiral is spinning again as a metallic voice echoes from the speaker. Professor Forster said this was impossible. Buzz is back, and it's talking to me.

I shake my head, trying to make sense of how this can be happening as my thoughts tumble and whirl.

"Who is Dad?" Buzz repeats, the robotic voice sounding softer, almost human now.

I take a deep breath. If this really is an alien civilization on the other end of the line, I've got to make sure I give the right answer. The fate of the human race could depend on what I say. It could mean the difference between invasion and an invitation to join the Galactic Federation.

With a trembling finger, I tap on the phone screen to bring up my camera then flick through the gallery of pictures until I find the one I'm looking for.

"This is my family," I tell Buzz. "Mom and Dad, Charlie and me."

In the picture Dad is standing with one arm around Mom, smiles beaming from both their faces as a fairy-tale castle sparkles with light behind them. I'm holding Dad's other hand looking up at the camera with a huge grin as Mom cradles baby Charlotte in her arms. This photo was taken at Disney World in Florida on Dad's day off from his training on the Light Swarm launch simulator at the

Kennedy Space Center. It's my favorite picture of us all together.

Without my touching it, the photo suddenly zooms until Dad's face fills the screen. I can see every detail of his smile, his sunny features unlined with worry. He looks so happy—just like the rest of us. I search his eyes for any trace of doubt—looking for a sign that could explain what's gone wrong, but I can't see a thing.

"Where is your dad?" Buzz asks.

Outside my bedroom window, the sky is ink black with a blanket of stars scattered across it. I hold the phone up to the open window.

"He's up there," I say sadly, scanning the sky for any sign of the International Space Station.

For a second, the low hum of the phone's vibration seems to quiet as if Buzz is looking out from the camera lens. Then I hear the soft tone of its voice again.

"That is where we come from too."

As I hold the phone up, I see a new picture appear on the screen, pale pinpricks of light studding the sky above Beacon Hill. I recognize the shapes of the different constellations Dad showed me when we stargazed together on nights like this: Pisces and Pegasus, Cygnus the swan, and Aquila the eagle with the bright star of Altair shining from its head. When Dad first taught me how to look at the stars, I could never quite see the shapes of the animals and people that gave the constellations their names. We'd spend hours tracing their shapes in the sky, while Dad told me incredible stories about Greek myths and gods. But now as I look at the Archer with his bow drawn low over the horizon, these shapes Dad showed me are all I can see.

"From the stars . . ."

As I stare at my cell phone, the shapes of these constellations suddenly shatter into pieces. I watch, amazed, as the stars begin racing toward the screen, pinpricks of pure white light erupting into brilliant blue flares and then fading to a red glow at the edge of the screen, again and again and again. It's like some out-of-control spaceship is taking me on a tour of the galaxy, traveling at the speed of light. I see clouds of dust and gas scattering into spirals and swirls as the emptiness of space surrounds me.

"We've traveled so very far."

In the center of the screen, I see a single pinprick of light grow larger before splitting into twin stars, these bright white sparks transformed into fiery spheres. In the shadow of the larger star, I see the shape of a planet in orbit, a blue-green world that almost looks like Earth.

"Is this where you come from?" I murmur, watching hypnotized as the blue-green planet fills the screen. As the camera swoops, I can't tear my gaze away from the bizarre alien landscape that's unfolding in front of me, so strange, yet strangely familiar too.

Twin suns shine in a bright purple sky above a vast forest filled with giant plants and ferns. Black flowers bloom in every direction, and rising above these are huge golden spirals, shimmering like trapped sunlight. These unearthly skyscrapers are exactly the same as the ones I drew in class today, but instead of pastel colors they now glisten in high definition. This impossible picture—these imaginary alien cities spiraling into the sky—it's all real.

"Home."

The soft vibration of Buzz's voice echoes inside my head. As the camera twists, the screen seems to blur as it circles around this enormous alien structure. It looks as if it's made of liquid metal, its golden surface pulsing as a swarm of creatures rises up into the sky. The sound of their beating wings buzzes from the phone as behind them on the screen I watch the sun being pulled apart by an invisible hand.

The picture slowly fades to black as the phone stops vibrating. I jab my finger against the screen—not wanting this weird science-fiction film to end. It's like my cell phone has suddenly got a billion-dollar special effects budget and I can't wait to find out what happens next.

But the only thing that appears is the golden spiral on my home screen, the icon now spinning soundlessly.

"Was that you?" I ask, the blurry image of those alien creatures frozen in my mind. I should feel scared, but somehow I know that Buzz doesn't mean me any harm.

"We are the Hi'ive."

The golden spiral pulses in time with the sound of Buzz's voice. The robotic tone that I heard when Buzz first started speaking has completely disappeared now. I can't tell whether I'm speaking to a man or a woman, but does that even mean anything when you're talking to an alien?

"If you're an alien," I ask, trying to make sense of the impossible, "how do you even understand English?"

The phone begins to vibrate in my hand, jumping like a flea with every buzz. I see countless texts scrolling across the screen, almost too fast to read. It looks like every text I've ever sent or received all scrolling by in the blink of an eye. A babble of voice-mail messages erupts from the speaker, the sound blurring into a single buzzing whine.

"We are the Hi'ive," Buzz replies. "We learn."

I stare at the phone, my head ready to explode. But before I can ask another question, my bedroom door starts to open, and I quickly shove my buzzing cell phone under my pillow.

"What are you looking at?" Charlie asks as she peers around the door. "Is it rude?"

"No," I say, my face flushing red all the same. I switch on my bedside lamp, Charlie taking this as a green light to shuffle into my room. "What are you doing out of bed anyway? You were supposed to be asleep ages ago."

Charlie's wearing her Peppa Pig pajamas, and, as she climbs on to my bed next to me, I can tell that she's been crying.

"What's the matter?" I ask, putting my arm around Charlie's shoulder as she hugs her favorite teddy close to her chest. Dad gave this to Charlie just before he took off for the International Space Station. The cuddly bear is dressed in a bright silver space suit, and Dad named it Teddy Gagarin, but Charlie just calls it Teddy Gaga now. "Are you okay?"

"I had a bad dream," Charlie replies with a snuffle, wiping her nose with the bear's furry paw. "I dreamed that aliens stole Daddy's spaceship and he couldn't find his way home."

She looks up at me, her cheeks still blotchy and red.

"I want Daddy," she sobs, breaking into tears again. "I want him home now."

From upstairs I can hear the sound of Mom moving things around in her attic studio. Usually this would be my cue to shout upstairs and let Mom come and deal with Charlie. But after our argument, I don't think that's a good idea. I need to try something else to distract her.

"Hey," I say, lifting Teddy Gagarin's paw to wipe Charlie's tears away. "Do you think Teddy Gaga would let any aliens steal Dad's spaceship?"

"No," Charlie sniffs.

"No," I agree. "And you know what he'd do if they tried? He'd beat them up—just like this." Waggling his arms, I show how Teddy Gagarin would throw some furry kung fu moves to fight off the aliens. "Douf! Douf! Douf!"

Charlie giggles.

"So you don't need to worry about Dad getting lost in space. He'll be back home next week to tell you and Teddy all about his adventures."

I get up from the bed, reaching my hands out to Charlie before lifting her down.

"Come on," I say. "Let's get you back to bed before Teddy Gaga goes kung fu gaga."

Charlie holds my hand as I lead her across the landing back to her bedroom. Through a crack in the curtains, the moon throws soft shadows over her Winnie-the-Pooh wallpaper. As she climbs into bed, I can see the fat yellow bear floating through the sky above her head. A bit like Dad, really, although the ISS has solar panels instead of a blue balloon like Winnie-the-Pooh.

Deep inside, I feel the same surge of emotion that fueled Charlie's tears. I wish Dad was home too, but if he and Mom are really splitting up, I don't know how long he'll stay. . . .

With her head on her pillow, Charlie looks up at me with her big brown eyes.

"Aliens aren't real, are they, Jamie?" she says, her nightmare now fading in the glow from her Peppa Pig night-light.

"No," I lie as I tuck her in under the covers. "You don't need to worry about aliens."

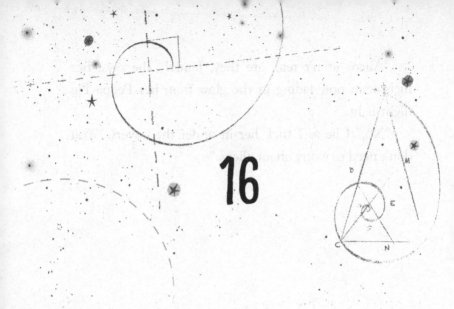

16

"SO, DAN, IN JUST OVER TWENTY-FOUR HOURS' TIME YOU will be stepping out of the International Space Station to space walk to the Lux Aeterna launch platform. There, you will launch the Light Swarm probes, sending those tiny spaceships on a hundred-trillion-kilometer trip to the stars in search of alien life. How are you feeling?"

The camera cuts from the glossy-haired presenter on the breakfast TV sofa to my dad on board the International Space Station. He's floating in exactly the same place as where I spoke to him yesterday, holding one finger to his ear as he waits to hear the question.

"Daddy!" Charlie throws her arms up in excitement at

the sight of Dad on the TV screen. Her left hand catches the edge of her bowl of porridge, flipping it up into the air before gravity drops its contents all over Granddad.

"Oh, Charlie," Mom says, grabbing a cloth from the kitchen sink as the porridge bowl clatters to a halt at her feet. Granddad looks down at his Death Panda T-shirt—Charlie's porridge splats giving the cartoon panda on the front a messy makeover. Shocked by the launch of her UFP—Unexpected Flying Porridge—Charlie bursts into tears, and I have to strain my ears to catch Dad's reply.

"I feel very proud," he says, a slight buzzing echo on his words as they bounce around the world. "Everyone has worked so hard to make this mission a success. From the scientists and engineers back at home who developed and built the Light Swarm technology to all the astronauts who constructed the orbital launch platform. I'm just a small cog in a much larger machine, but I feel hugely honored that when I press that button at the launch platform tomorrow, I will be helping the human race to take our first step to the stars."

"And how do you think your family will be feeling now?" the presenter asks as the time delay kicks in again.

I should be feeling proud too, but instead I just feel so resentful. It seems like Dad's more bothered about being a famous astronaut now than he is about being a dad. I look around the kitchen table. Mom's giving Charlie a hug, my little sister still sobbing as Granddad tries to de-porridge his T-shirt with the wet cloth. Maybe family life just isn't exciting enough for him.

"I think they might be a little nervous," Dad finally replies. "But hopefully they're all feeling proud of me."

"We all are, Dan," the TV presenter says with a smile. "There's only ten seconds left on the satellite, so we've got to let you go now, but everyone here wishes you the very best of luck with your mission tomorrow." With a final wave, the picture of my dad disappears from the screen to be replaced by a weather map. "And to find out whether it will be bright and sunny for Dan's space walk, let's hear the forecast from Clare."

Reaching for the remote, Mom switches off the TV, prompting a fresh howl from Charlie.

"Come on, silly," Mom says, giving Charlie a cuddle as she lifts her out of her chair. "Your dad will be home soon." She looks across at me as I push my own chair back from the table. "Do you want a lift to school, Jamie, after I've dropped Charlie off at nursery?"

Feeling the faint buzz of my cell phone in the depths of my pocket, I quickly shake my head. If Mom gets me in the car on my own, she'll just start talking about the divorce, and that's the last thing I want to think about now.

"No thanks. I'd rather walk today."

I haven't had the chance to look at my phone properly since it went all intergalactic on me last night. When I got back to my room after putting Charlie to bed, Buzz seemed to have shut down. Now as I near the school gates with my cell phone in my hand, my thumb hovers over the spiral icon, just waiting for it to start spinning again.

To be honest, I didn't sleep much last night. In science-fiction films, there are usually two types of aliens. There are the cute, cuddly ones like E.T. who just want to get back home to their own planet, and then there're the bug-eyed aliens who blow up the White House and take over the world. Now, I'm really hoping that Buzz is the first type, but the thing is, there are tons more movies made about evil alien invaders and, technically, Buzz has hijacked my phone. . . .

"BZZZ."

Flinching in surprise, I glance down at the screen. The golden spiral is spinning again, its unfurling loop growing wider with every turn. As Buzz's voice hums from the speaker, I feel an answering buzz in my brain.

"Synchronizing. BZZZ."

"What do you mean?" I ask, feeling slightly panicked as the tip of my finger flickers brightly beneath the sunlight. "What's happening to me?"

"We are connected." Buzz's voice echoes inside my head. "It is time for you to learn about the Hi'ive."

For a second, I stare at my phone, dumbfounded. The golden spiral is still spinning, but my eyes can't seem to focus on it. It feels as though I'm looking at the screen through a piece of wire gauze—just like the ones we use in science class—but this one's tinted gold. I blink, trying to clear my vision, but when I open them again, my heart skips a beat.

On the screen, I can see a huge golden spiral reaching up into a purple sky, but then the picture shifts and suddenly I'm plunging into its heart.

I can almost feel the pressure of the onrushing air, the picture spiraling dizzily as it swoops through a thick golden haze. My ears pop, the sound of the humming inside my head suddenly louder. Beneath my fingers, my phone feels sticky as I watch the screen seem to expand and my vision fills with the most unbelievable sight.

I'm hanging suspended in a cathedral of light, a vast space filled with endless rows of hexagonal cells spiraling in every direction. Each cell gleams with an unearthly glow, its golden light flickering to the hum of a billion buzzing voices lifted up in what sounds like a prayer.

I feel Buzz's presence flickering in my mind.

"We are old—so much older than you. And we know so much."

I'm not just seeing this anymore—it's like I'm inside a liquid gold hive, or maybe it's inside of me. For a second, I almost forget to breathe and feel like I'm drowning in an ocean of light, every particle humming with information. I catch glimpses of the impossible reflected in the light, ideas so far beyond my understanding I can't even begin to put them into words.

That's when I realize: *this* is the Hi'ive. Everything they've ever said. Everything they've ever done. Everything they've ever known. Their art, their science, their stories, their songs—all trapped inside this shimmering light.

"We are many and we are one. The living and the dead and the yet to come. We are the Hi'ive."

The humming sound surrounds me now, so beautiful and strange. It's like the air itself is an invisible library, the books filled with sunlight.

That's when I see them: a swarm of strange alien creatures dancing toward the light. Just like before, I can't quite make out their features, only their silvery wings beating against the shimmering air. I watch as they whirl in spiraling circles, their every movement pulsing through the vast structure until it vibrates with an unstoppable energy.

"This is what we were." Buzz's voice hums inside my head. **"Frail creatures of muscle and brain, so vulnerable to**

harm. We had learned so much, harnessing the energy of the stars, but then the darkness came."

I don't know which way is up or down anymore—my head is spinning as Buzz's voice fills my brain. But at the summit of this spiraling hive of light, there's an open circle of sky. Through this I can see a giant sun, its golden sphere slowly being shredded into blazing jets of gas. It's as if it's being devoured by some invisible predator, flailing in its death throes as the sky turns black.

"The Hi'ive had to choose. Our bodies or our minds. There was no choice."

At the center of the vast structure, I see a golden beam stretching up to the stars. The alien creatures spiral in perfect circles as they ascend into the heart of the shimmering beacon, their bodies surrendering to its brilliance until they can no longer be seen.

"We went into the light," Buzz sings.

My mind reels as this golden light surrounds me too.

"And then we swarmed."

Suddenly I feel myself catapulted across space. It's as if the intergalactic tour that Buzz gave me last night is now running backward, flares of light endlessly erupting and being extinguished in the blink of an eye. I see planets, asteroids, comets, and satellites whizzing past, before I catch a glimpse of the Hubble Space Telescope, its solar panels angled toward the sun as the giant eye of its lens fills the screen. I wince, waiting for an impact that never comes as the golden light spins through a whirling hall of mirrors before finally tumbling into darkness.

Blinking in surprise, I open my eyes to find that I'm standing outside the school gates. The phone is still in my hand, the golden spiral slowly turning as Buzz speaks again.

"We are the Hi'ive. We survived."

"It wasn't real," I murmur, unable to shift the image of the aliens dancing to their deaths as the light swallowed them whole. That same light racing across the universe until it hit the Hubble Space Telescope.

"We are as real as you are," Buzz replies, the words softly buzzing from my phone. **"We have just moved beyond the limits of the physical world. Inside every atom in the universe is a fireball of light, a constant flow of photons that keeps every particle intact. This is where we live now—where our minds still thrive. We are creatures of the light. We are the Hi'ive."**

My head is spinning with everything I've seen and heard, but it all makes a peculiar kind of sense now. Professor Forster was wrong. When that light hit the Hubble Space Telescope, it wasn't a signal or some kind of message from the stars—it was the Hi'ive. Their entire civilization beamed across trillions of kilometers of space until it finally struck Hubble's mirror. And as the sensors at the heart of the telescope transmitted this signal to the Laser Optical Ground Station that was hooked up to Professor Forster's laptop—that was the moment I plugged my phone in.

This alien intelligence was downloaded to my cell phone. An extraterrestrial civilization stored on my SD card. All their knowledge, all their wisdom, all their cleverness is now sitting next to my contacts on the home screen.

"What do you want?" I murmur.

"Help. BZZZ."

"Who are you talking to?"

At the sound of Minty's voice, I turn in surprise and then nearly jump out of my skin as I see a green bug-eyed alien staring back at me.

114

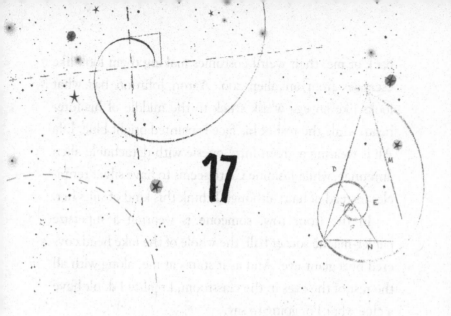

17

THE GOOD NEWS IS THAT MINTY'S NOT MUTATED INTO AN alien lizard queen who wants to take over the world. She's just wearing a costume. The bad news is that I've forgotten to do my homework, unlike the rest of my class, who are now all dressed up like monsters out of *Doctor Who*.

"So, Jamie," Mrs. Solomon says, casting a disappointed look over my school uniform as I stand in front of her desk. "I can see you've decided not to create your own intergalactic costume, but I'd still like you to tell us all about the aliens that you've invented. What kind of extraterrestrial species do *you* think your dad's space probes might discover?"

Nervously, I look up to see the rest of the class staring

back at me, their weird costumes making them look like escapees from an alien zoo. Aaron Johnson has what looks like an egg whisk stuck to the middle of his forehead, while the rest of his face is painted bright blue. Lila Ali is wearing a green furry onesie with detachable alien antennae, while Jasmine Clark seems to have silver tentacles instead of hair, although I think this kind of suits her.

In the front row, someone is wearing a supersize papier-mâché soccer ball, the whole of the fake head covered by a giant eye. And as it stares at me, along with all the rest of the eyes in the classroom, I realize I don't have a clue what I'm going to say.

I'm usually pretty good at getting my homework done, but with everything that's been going on, I haven't had the time to invent some make-believe alien. I've got enough problems working out what to do with this real one that's shown up on my phone. I slip my hand into my pocket, my fingers closing around my phone as I squeeze it tight, hoping that Buzz can pull another alien mind trick to magic me out of this hole.

But the phone stays silent. It looks like this time, I'm on my own.

"When you're ready, Jamie," Mrs. Solomon prompts me. "You have done your homework, haven't you?"

Next to my empty chair, Minty grins, her green lizard face lighting up at the sight of my embarrassment.

There's only one thing I can do. Tell the truth.

"The aliens that I've discovered," I start to explain, "are called the Hi'ive." And then it all pours out of me—everything I've found out, everything Buzz has shown me. Using the picture I drew, I tell the class about their huge spiral cities filled with golden light, the air teeming with alien intelligence. I talk about the swarms of satellites they use to harness the power of the stars. I explain how the Hi'ive have lived for billions of years and how they survived.

And when I finally stop talking, I see my teacher staring back at me, her mouth open wide. I glance around at the faces of my classmates, their alien disguises unable to hide their surprise as Minty slowly shakes her head to let me know I've gone too far.

"Wow," Mrs. Solomon says when she finally remembers to speak. "I wasn't expecting that. You've thought of everything, Jamie—how your alien civilization would live, the technologies they might develop, but most importantly how they would communicate. A hive mind storing the knowledge of their entire species—living beings transformed into pure energy traveling across the galaxy at the speed of light. It's an incredible thought."

But the rest of her gushing praise is swiftly cut off as the school bell rings.

As everyone starts talking at once, our teacher claps her hands.

"That's not the bell for break time, Class Six," she

explains, raising her voice above the hubbub. "We're having a special assembly today in the school hall and that's where I want you to go now."

With a groan, the rest of the class start to wriggle their costumes out of their seats as they head toward the door. But as I turn to join them, Mrs. Solomon calls me back.

"Jamie, could I have a quick word?"

At first I think she's going to give me a hard time for not dressing up like an alien, but then I spot my math test on the desk in front of her.

"I know that you have struggled a little with your math work this term," my teacher begins, fixing me with a sympathetic smile, "but I wanted to talk to you about this test paper."

"I'm sorry I tried to use my calculator," I say quickly, thinking that Mrs. Solomon is going to mark me down for cheating or something.

Mrs. Solomon shakes her head.

"It's not that, Jamie. It's your answer to the last question that I wanted to ask you about." She turns over my test paper to reveal the scribbled letters, symbols, and numbers that cover the page. "You see, most of the class stuck to inventing simple linear equations, but you seemed to get a little carried away."

I look down at the scrawled equation. I don't even remember writing this.

"I was just messing about, Miss."

"That's what I thought," Mrs. Solomon replies. "But I've had a friend staying with me this week who works as a professor of particle physics at Lancaster University. She's currently running a project at the Deep Mine Lab over in Clackthorpe. My friend happened to spot your test paper and said that your equation looked a lot like the standard model."

"What's that?" I ask, starting to feel confused. I don't know how my messy scribble can look anything like a model equation.

"The standard model of particle physics," Mrs. Solomon replies. She frowns as if trying to work out exactly what to say. "It's a little difficult for me to explain, as I'm not an expert, but according to my friend, it's the theory that explains how the universe works."

I look again at the scribbled lines of letters and numbers. I didn't know the universe came with instructions, but these look even more confusing than the ones that came with Charlie's build-it-yourself dresser, and Dad spent the whole weekend assembling that.

"So how did you come to write this equation on your test, Jamie?" Mrs. Solomon asks, her forehead wrinkling into a frown. "My friend says she only teaches this to her masters students and didn't think that a primary school pupil would've even heard of the standard model."

She's right about that, but I bet Buzz has.

"I must have seen it somewhere," I reply, desperately trying to think up an excuse that doesn't include the alien on my phone. "Maybe it was in one of my dad's books. It must have just stuck in my head."

"I thought that'd be it," Mrs. Solomon says, a sigh of relief washing the frown from her face. "I told my friend that your dad was Dan Drake—astronaut and all-around genius. The funny thing is, you made a mistake in the equation anyway." She points halfway down the page, and following her fingertip, I see the letter "G" scribbled in the margin. "My friend thought at first that you'd included gravity in the equation, but the thing is, scientists haven't worked out how to fit this into their theory of everything."

She looks up at me with a smile.

"You got my friend excited for a minute, though, Jamie. She thought I had the next Albert Einstein in my class."

Dad says it's gravity that keeps the International Space Station spinning around the world. Well, if Mrs. Solomon's friend is right, maybe the Hi'ive have worked out how it keeps the universe spinning too.

"Mrs. Solomon!"

The booming sound of the principal's voice makes me jump in surprise.

"We're all ready for you in the hall now," Mr. Hayes announces, peering around the classroom door. "So if you'd like to bring our special guest along."

I look around in confusion. The rest of the class have already gone. Apart from me and Mrs. Solomon, there's nobody else here, unless my teacher has hidden this mystery guest inside her stock cupboard.

"Come on, Jamie," Mrs. Solomon says. "It's time for assembly."

And that's when I realize he's talking about me.

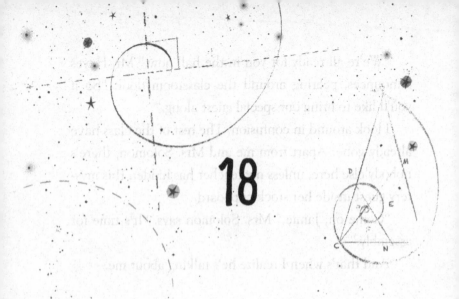

18

SITTING ON THE SIDE OF THE STAGE NEXT TO MRS. SOLOMON and Mr. Hayes, I look out at the rest of the school. The hall is packed, every class sitting crossed-legged on the floor, while the teachers huddle around the edges. It's easy to spot my class sitting halfway down on the right. In their alien costumes, they look like a band of extra-terrestrial bounty hunters who've beamed down to school by mistake, marooned in a sea of royal-blue school uniforms.

In the front row, the littlest kids are bouncing up and down with excitement, pointing up at the stage as they talk among themselves. But I'm not the person they're excited to see. He's on the huge projector screen that has descended from the ceiling to fill most of the stage.

I glance up at this to see my dad floating on the ISS.

"Hello, Austen Park Primary. This is Commander Dan Drake, and I'd like to welcome you all aboard the International Space Station."

Everyone starts clapping and cheering, their excited whoops filling the hall with noise. I didn't know any of this was happening until I got to the school hall. Hayley Collins was waiting for me there and explained how Dad was feeling bad about missing my birthday on Friday, so they'd set up this live link as a birthday surprise.

Raising his hands, Mr. Hayes gestures for quiet.

"So," the principal says, speaking into the microphone that's transmitting his words to the ISS, "who's got the first question for Jamie's dad?"

A forest of hands shoots up across the hall.

"Your class teachers have all got roving microphones so that Commander Drake can hear your questions. So if you're picked to ask a question, wait until you've got hold of the microphone before you start to speak."

Mr. Hayes drops his gaze onto the front row. A little kid with curly black hair looks like he's trying to pull his own arm out of its socket, thrusting his hand as high as it will go in his desperation to get picked.

"Let's start with a question from Miss Brightman's

class. Harrison, isn't it?" As his face lights up with excitement, the boy nods, and Miss Brightman rushes to hand him her roving microphone. "Don't forget, it's a long way up to the International Space Station, so speak as loudly and clearly as you can."

Harrison wraps both his hands around the microphone, staring up in wonder at my dad on the projector screen. That's when I realize I recognize this little kid. It's the baby alien boy who stopped me in the corridor on Monday morning, and I instantly know what question he's going to ask.

"How do you go to the bathroom in space?"

Everyone starts laughing, even Mr. Hayes. There's a two-second delay, and then Dad joins in too.

"That's a very good question, Harrison," he says, trying to pretend he hasn't been asked this a million times before. Dad lets go of his microphone for a second, letting this float in front of him. "As you can see, the microgravity up here can make going to the bathroom a little tricky. Luckily, the toilets on the International Space Station use suction, a bit like your vacuum cleaner at home, to make sure we don't end up with any unpleasant floaters." Dad grabs hold of his microphone again. "But on my space walk tomorrow, I'll be wearing maximum absorbency underpants just in case I need to pee."

I sink down in my chair as everyone laughs again.

Now the whole school knows that my dad will be wearing a space diaper tomorrow.

Luckily, that's the only question about Dad's toilet habits as Mr. Hayes fields the questions from the rest of the school.

"What's it like being weightless all the time?"

"What do you eat and drink on the space station?"

"What can you see out of the window right now?"

And Dad answers them all, talking about how great it is to be in space and showing off some of the cool things he can do in microgravity along the way, like spinning a space somersault, drinking water droplets out of the air, and playing with the yo-yo that I bought him for Christmas.

"Let's take a couple of questions from Jamie's classmates now," Mr. Hayes says, his gaze landing on the alien outpost of Class Six. "What do you want to ask, Aaron?"

Aaron lowers his Dalek plunger as our teaching assistant, Miss Tyler, hands him a microphone.

"What would happen if you forgot to put your space suit on before your space walk tomorrow?" he asks.

There's the usual two-second delay before Dad begins his reply.

"Well," he says, "my space suit is really more of a spaceship. It's called an Extravehicular Mobility Unit—or EMU, for short. The life-support backpack gives me eight hours of oxygen, and the rocket propulsion system of the Advanced Manned Maneuvering Unit that fits over the EMU will transport me safely to the higher orbit of the Lux Aeterna launch platform. Inside my helmet, there's a communication system that lets me talk to Mission Control and a built-in video camera that lets them see exactly what I'm doing."

"But what would happen if you forgot to put this on?" Aaron interrupts, the egg whisk stuck to his head wobbling as he keeps a tight hold on the microphone.

There's a burst of static as Dad's and Aaron's voices overlap, which gives Miss Tyler the chance to wrestle the microphone out of Aaron's grasp. Then Dad's voice fills the hall again.

"Well, space is a dangerous place. There's cosmic radiation to contend with, the temperature can veer from one hundred and twenty degrees Celsius to minus one hundred and fifty degrees in the shade, and without any air to breathe in the vacuum of space, I'd probably suffocate in about fifteen seconds flat."

I shift uneasily in my seat, suddenly wishing I was anywhere but here.

"Let's have another question," Mr. Hayes says brightly. "What do you want to ask, Araminta?"

Taking the microphone in her lizard claw, Minty fixes my dad with a bug-eyed glare.

"Can I go on one of the Light Swarm spaceships?" she demands. "I want to meet the aliens."

Up on the big screen, a huge grin spreads over Dad's face.

"Looking at the pictures your teachers have sent me of your intergalactic outfits, I thought I'd made contact with aliens already. But I'm afraid you wouldn't be able to hitch a ride back to your home planet on one of the Light Swarm probes."

Dad reaches out of shot to pick something up, and when he reappears on the screen, I see he's holding what looks like a silver postage stamp in the palm of his hand. I recognize this immediately as one of the Light Swarm probes.

"You see, these tiny spacecraft are only one centimeter long and there's just no space for anyone to hitch a ride." With a delicate touch, Dad slides out a tiny black chip from the heart of the probe. It looks just like any SD card that you'd find inside your phone. "This wafer-size chip weighs less than a gram but contains all of the probe's cameras, its communications system, and its power source. When I reach the HabZone module of the Lux Aeterna launch platform tomorrow, I'll make sure that all these chips are fitted to the Light Swarm probes before I press the button to send them on a hundred-and-eight-trillion-kilometer trip to Tau Ceti."

The school hall is silent now as everyone stares at this interstellar spaceship that fits into the palm of Dad's hand.

"Of course it's not just my space walk that I've got marked on my calendar tomorrow," Dad continues, placing the probe out of shot. "There's another reason that it's a special day." As he reappears on the screen I can see that he's holding a gift-wrapped box. "I think there's just time for one final question."

This is my cue. Hayley has explained everything to me, and she's now standing in the wings on the other side of the stage, holding the same gift-wrapped box in her arms. As Mr. Hayes hands me the microphone I know exactly what I'm supposed to say, the words written down on a scrap of paper just in case I forget.

Hey, Dad, it's Jamie—what have you
got me for my birthday?

Then Dad's going to wish me happy birthday for tomorrow and Hayley will walk out to give me my birthday present. When she saw how worried I was looking, Hayley couldn't stop herself from telling me what's under the wrapping paper. It's a Lego model of the International Space Station and Lux Aeterna launch platform. It even comes with a minifigure of my dad in his EMU space suit.

Hayley says it's one of a kind. It should be the best birthday present ever, but as I look up at Dad on the projector screen I feel a sudden surge of anger.

Is this what life is going to be like now? Sharing my dad with a roomful of strangers and getting my birthday presents secondhand? Having everyone think that Dad's some kind of superhero, when really he's tearing our family apart?

I grip the microphone more tightly, my knuckles whitening as I stare up at Dad's smile.

"Are you there, Jamie?" he asks, a slight echo on his words as they fill the school hall.

Mr. Hayes clears his throat to let my dad know that the satellite link is still working. From the other side of the stage, Hayley shoots me a worried look, her arms sagging slightly under the weight of the Lego box.

A faint buzz from the phone in my pocket reminds me that Dad doesn't know everything, after all. There's a lump in my throat the size of a small planet, and as I fight back my tears, I know the question I've got to ask.

"If it's so great being an astronaut, why don't you just stay up there?"

It takes two seconds for my question to reach Dad on the ISS, so before he even has the chance to answer, I drop the microphone and run off the stage.

"Jamie!"

I hear Hayley and my teachers calling me back, then the sound of Dad's voice crashing through the speakers.

"Jamie, are you okay?"

But I keep on running—out of the hall and past the empty classrooms, out through the door and across the playground, out the school gates and down the street—not stopping until I finally run out of breath.

I can't stop myself from crying as I stare up into the clear blue sky. Through my tears, I see the sun shining down uncaringly. According to Mrs. Solomon, the light that's now hitting my eyes left the surface of the sun eight minutes and twenty seconds ago. That was probably when Dad was showing off his yo-yo tricks on the ISS. Before I told him he should just stay in space if he was having so much fun up there. What's the point of him coming home if he's not planning to stay?

I feel my cell phone vibrating in my pocket, the muffled sound of Buzz's voice calling out to me. I pull it out to see the golden spiral on the home screen spinning frantically.

"Jamie!" Buzz's voice sounds almost anxious. **"There's a storm coming."**

With a hollow laugh, I hold the phone up to the bright blue sky.

"Don't be stupid," I say. "There's not a cloud in sight."

But before Buzz can speak again, my cell phone starts ringing.

I look down at the caller display and see three letters there.

DAD

With a fresh surge of fury, I stab my finger against the power button. The ringtone cuts out as the screen fades to black.

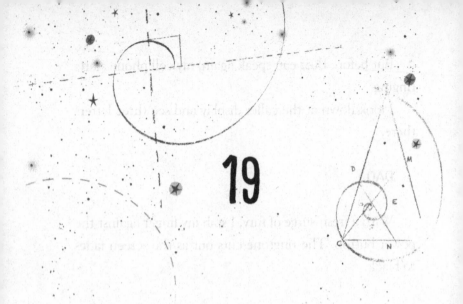

19

"SO THIS IS WHERE YOU'VE GOT TO."

Granddad's hands rest on my shoulders as I sit on the back wall, my school shoes scuffing the flower heads as I stare across the meadow to the foot of Beacon Hill.

"The school has been on the phone. Your mom's worried sick. She's out in the car with Charlie looking for you now. We've all been calling your cell phone."

Shaking his hands from my shoulders, I swing myself down from the wall.

"I switched my phone off," I tell him, quickly wiping my eyes so he can't see that I've been crying. "I just needed some time to think."

"Oh, Jamie lad," Granddad says, his voice softening as his big arms envelop me in a bear hug. His sticky T-shirt smells of porridge and stale cigarettes. "Come into the barn and let's have a proper chat."

Sitting on an upturned beer crate, I look around at the chaos that clutters the barn, most of the space filled with the wreckage of Granddad's rock-star past. Towering amplifiers and monitors line the walls, each one stenciled with the Death Panda logo. Leaning against these are electric guitars of every size, shape, and color, while leads and cables snake across the sticky floor. A flame-red drum kit is set up against the far wall, a cartoon panda bursting out of the front of the large bass drum.

"This used to be our rehearsal space when the band was still together," Granddad says as he strides across the floor. "But since the band broke up it's become a bit of a dumping ground. That's why I let your mom work on her new sculpture in here, to brighten the place up. Plus she couldn't fit it up the stairs to the attic."

He points across the room to where four separate columns of glass and steel rise at least three meters high. The tall curving shapes seem to twist and curl together, their colored glass filling the room with light.

Before Charlie was born, I remember Dad taking me to watch Mom work at her studio. I remember her face fixed in concentration as she conjured strange creatures out of the glass, their shapes changing from whichever angle you looked. I remember Mom and Dad laughing together as I tried to guess what animal each sculpture was supposed to be—a rabbit, a pony, a unicorn, a dragon— their laughs getting louder as my guesses got more ridiculous. And now I don't know if I'll ever hear them laugh together again.

Sitting down on the drum stool, Granddad picks up an electric guitar and with his bandaged hand *kerrangs* out an unamplified chord.

"I played this guitar at the Monsters of Rock festival back in eighty-two," he reminisces. "That was where I met your grandma for the first time. We were together for twenty-five years until she left with that bloody American drummer."

For a second Granddad just sits there with a faraway look in his eyes, his left hand stroking the neck of his guitar. Then he looks at me, the lines of his wrinkled face creasing into a frown.

"I heard you talking to your mom about the divorce yesterday."

I slump down farther in my makeshift seat, burying my head in my hands. All the anger I felt when I was standing onstage in front of Dad on that huge projector screen has faded away. All that's left now is the pain.

"I don't know why they're splitting up," I say, the words almost catching in my throat. "I don't know who's to blame. I've waited so long for Dad to come home, and now Mom says we can't be together anymore. Why can't they just work things out?"

Granddad absentmindedly strums his guitar, the unamplified notes ringing out a melancholy tune.

"Sometimes things just don't work out. Bands, marriages, record deals. People change and people move on. Your mom has put her life on hold for a long time to help your dad achieve his dreams, moving you from country to country and almost giving up on her career. Don't you think it's time that she has the chance to shine?"

"Can't she do that with Dad?"

Granddad shakes his head.

"It's not for me to say, Jamie. You really need to talk to your mom and dad. Together."

"But I can't," I say, fighting back my tears.

"I know," Granddad sighs, resting his guitar against the amp as he gets up from the drum stool. He walks across the barn to rest his hand on my shoulder. "Not yet. There's enough going on with your dad's space walk tomorrow. But you need to remember, Jamie, your mom and dad love you and Charlie, and that won't ever change."

I squeeze my eyes shut, remembering the last time I saw Dad properly. He was in quarantine at the spaceport in Kazakhstan, waiting for the Soyuz rocket to blast off for the International Space Station. Before launch, astronauts have to stay away from any potential sources of germs so they don't end up getting sick in space. So the last time I saw Dad face to face he was behind a sealed glass window, Dad holding up his hand to mine as he said goodbye. The same way he does now at the end of every video call.

Sitting on the upturned crate, I feel the weight of all my worries pushing me down—just like the g-forces on Dad when he blasted off into space. I've got an alien on my phone, and I don't know what's going to happen when Dad gets home. I just wish he were back right now.

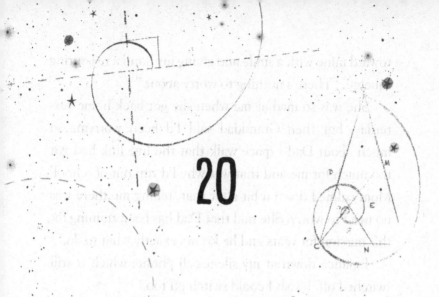

20

NESTLED ON THE SOFA BETWEEN MOM AND GRANDDAD, I stare at the TV. The picture is frozen, showing a blank blue screen as Hayley talks on the phone to Mission Control. I glance over at the clock on the wall. It's just past eight—time for Dad to set off on his space walk to the Lux Aeterna launch platform. My birthday cards are all lined up on the mantelpiece, but I'm saving opening my presents until Dad has completed his mission.

Charlie bounces up and down on Mom's knee.

"Where's Daddy?" she asks for what seems like the millionth time.

"He'll be there soon," Mom says, tilting her head

137

toward mine with a smile and giving my hand a reassuring squeeze. "There's nothing to worry about."

She was so mad at me when she got back home yesterday, but then Granddad said I'd been worrying so much about Dad's space walk that the live link had got too much for me and that was why I'd run out of school. Mom calmed down a bit after that, telling me there was no need to worry. She said that Dad has been training for this mission for years and he knows exactly what to do.

I glance down at my silent cell phone, which is still switched off. I wish I could switch off too.

Then Charlie screams excitedly as the blue screen disappears and is replaced with what looks like a handwritten sign. The picture is slightly blurry at first, but as this shifts into focus I can read the words written there.

Happy Birthday, Jamie!

The world is watching Dad's every move on this mega-important mission, but he's still found time to show he's thinking of me. My fingers tighten around my cell phone. Right now, I just wish I could call Dad and take back what I said yesterday, but I don't think he's free to pick up the phone.

On the sofa Mom gives me a hug, then Dad's astronaut glove lifts the sign out of shot, and we all gasp as the darkness of space fills the screen.

It's the blackest black I've ever seen, the inky darkness studded with thousands of stars. And in the center of the TV screen I can see the silver outline of the Lux Aeterna launch platform, its spiral of petallike panels facing out into the void.

Dad's voice crackles out of the TV speakers.

"Mission Control, this is Commander Drake. I'm clear of the ISS now and have visual on the Lux Aeterna platform. Request permission to engage the AMMU propulsion system to begin my ascent to its orbit."

With a burst of static, we hear Mission Control's reply on the radio.

"Copy that, Dan. Please ensure the Light Swarm probes are safely stowed before engaging propulsion system."

The picture on the screen shifts as Dad looks down and his helmet-cam shows the square silver case that's strapped to his space suit. Inside this are the Light Swarm probes, all ready to begin their 108-trillion-kilometer journey to Tau Ceti.

"All present and correct," Dad says, a slight buzz on his words as they echo across space. "I just hope we get some air miles with these probes, as they're taking a pretty big trip."

Next to me, Mom laughs at Dad's cheesy joke. Then I hear the smile in the voice of Mission Control's reply.

"Negative, Dan. No air miles, but they'll be flying

first-class with your help. Permission granted to engage propulsion system."

"Engaging primary thrusters."

The picture on the screen bobs slightly as we hear the whoosh of the propulsion system. At first I don't think it can be working properly, as the distant shape of the launch platform remains fixed in the center of the TV screen, but then I realize while the seconds tick by that it's growing ever so slightly larger against the background of stars. The change is so gradual that it feels to me like Dad is almost frozen in space, but then the spiral panels start to glint as the launch platform moves into sunlight, and I can tell that Dad is closer now.

In the background, I can hear a strange humming sound. I look down at my cell phone, but it's still switched off—I've got enough to worry about at the moment without Buzz piping up. But the buzzing noise from the TV is now a constant drone as Dad's helmet tilts, and I see for the first time the sleek silver module at the base of the launch platform. Dad's final destination.

I glance across at Hayley, who's standing watching with a look of concentration on her face.

"What's that buzzing noise?" I ask her.

Hayley smiles reassuringly.

"That's just the sound of the fan circulating oxygen through your dad's suit. Don't worry, Jamie—everything's going to plan."

"That's a relief," says Granddad, fiddling with his ear. "I thought this hearing aid was playing up again."

Then Dad's voice crackles over the radio.

"I've got visual on the HabZone air lock. Estimated rendezvous in approximately twelve minutes."

"Copy that, Dan. All systems' diagnostics are green— looking good for rendezvous."

I can see the circular air lock at the end of the Hab-Zone module, its porthole window staring back at me like a tiny silver face surrounded by the darkness of space.

Mom's holding my hand tightly now, Charlie sitting absolutely still on her knee. As we listen to the sound of Dad's breathing over the radio and watch the Lux Aeterna launch platform slowly fill the screen, we all just stare at the TV, spellbound.

Once Dad gets inside the launch platform module, he'll perform the final checks on the Light Swarm probes. Each tiny spacecraft will be slid into the delivery system that will propel them into position, ready for Dad to press the button that will fire the Lux Aeterna laser and launch them to the stars.

Dad's voice comes over the radio again.

"Rendezvous in five minutes."

He's closing in on the air lock now, the petallike shapes of the launch platform's solar panels disappear- ing from view as the HabZone module fills the screen entirely. I catch a glimpse of Dad's face reflected in its silvered surface, his astronaut's helmet framed by the blue of the world below.

My heart thumps in my chest. Dad's on top of the world, and I feel so proud.

His voice crackles out of the speaker again.

"Engaging retro thrusters."

I hear another whooshing sound—two quick blasts followed by a softer swooshing noise, the picture on the screen tilting as Dad's space suit brakes kick in to slow his approach. But as the air lock door fills the screen, the voice of Mission Control crackles from the speaker.

"Mission abort. Repeat. Mission abort. Initiate emergency protocols for shelter in event of systems failure."

Charlie turns toward Mom with a puzzled frown.

"What's a 'mer-jen-sea'?"

From the TV speaker comes a burst of static, and then we hear Dad's reply.

"Everything's fine here." Dad's breathing sounds slightly labored as he reaches out to turn the air lock handle. "All systems normal. Mission Control, can you elaborate?"

"Urgent warning received from the Space Weather Prediction Center in Colorado. They're reporting an X-class solar flare heading straight toward Earth."

The voice of Mission Control usually sounds so calm, but as these words echo across space I'm sure I can hear a note of panic.

I look across to Hayley for reassurance, but all the color seems to have suddenly drained from her face as she stares at the TV screen.

Dad is now trying to open the air lock's hatch, his bulky astronaut gloves grappling with the release handle.

"Do we have an ETA on that solar flare?" he asks, grunting out the words as he turns the handle clockwise.

"Negative. The NASA ACE satellite has been completely destroyed by the flare. You need to get inside the HabZone now!"

"What's going on?" Mom says, casting a panicked look in Hayley's direction as Charlie fidgets on her lap.

"It's a solar storm," Hayley replies, her gaze still fixed to the television. "A bad one. An X-class solar flare is an eruption of super-heated particles from the Sun's upper atmosphere, traveling toward Earth at almost the speed of light."

I grip my cell phone tightly in my hand. Buzz said there was a storm coming, but I didn't listen . . .

On the TV screen, the air lock hatch starts to swing open.

"Copy that, Mission Control. Initiating emergency—"

Then the picture freezes, Dad's voice suddenly silenced and replaced by a dead dial tone.

Charlie wails.

"Where's Daddy?"

As Mom hugs her tight, I turn toward Hayley, our family liaison now frantically tapping at her cell phone.

"Dad's going to be okay," I say, raising my voice above the sound of Charlie's crying. "He can just take shelter until the storm passes, can't he?"

Hayley looks up from her phone, her features set in a tight-lipped smile that doesn't fool me at all.

"That's what Mission Control has told him to do. Your dad will follow emergency protocols until the impact of the solar flare is known."

"I'm sure everything will be okay," Granddad says, resting his hand on my shoulder. "Your dad's trained for situations like this."

I look up at the TV screen, its frozen picture still showing the air lock door starting to open, but with Dad stuck outside in the vacuum of space. I remember exactly what he said when Aaron asked his stupid question yesterday: *"Space is a dangerous place."* Then the frozen image starts to break up, disintegrating in an avalanche of pixels before being replaced by a blank blue screen.

I feel a wave of nausea rising up in my throat, my stomach tumbling over and over as though I'm the one falling through space. Shaking Granddad's hand from my shoulder, I push myself up off the sofa.

"I feel sick. I need to get some fresh air."

Pressing my thumb against the power button on my

144

phone, I head for the door. Behind me I can hear Hayley talking to Mission Control while Mom tries to comfort Charlie. Running through the kitchen, I push the back door open, bright sunlight hitting my face as I step out into the garden.

Fighting to keep my breakfast down, I feel my phone vibrating in my hand. On the cell phone screen the golden spiral spins, and I hear Buzz's voice rise into the cloudless sky.

"The storm is here."

A shiver runs down my spine.

"How do you know?" I ask, holding up the phone as I stare at the sky. The sun looks just the same as it does every day—no sign of any solar storm—just gentle warmth shining down on my face.

"Your eyes only see a tiny fraction of the true light from your star," Buzz replies. "Less than a thousandth of one percent of the full spectrum of rays that shine down on your planet every day. But we are the Hi'ive and can see all the brightness that surrounds you."

On the screen of my phone a picture of the sky above me appears—the yellow-white sun suspended in a bright blue sky. But then I gasp as the sky on the screen suddenly comes alive with a kaleidoscope of colors. I see crimson and green streaks shooting in every direction, spirals of pink and orange eddying across the horizon. Purple halos spot the screen as these colors twist into strange new shapes. It's like when you rub your eyes when they're closed—colors bursting across my vision. But my eyes are wide open now. The sky is ablaze—burning with a rainbow of fire.

It looks like a video I saw of those strange lights that they get in the sky near the North Pole. The aurora borealis, or the northern lights. But those only come out at night and, as I lift my eyes from the phone, all I can see is broad daylight.

"What is this?" I murmur, my brain unable to process what Buzz is showing me on the screen.

"The solar flare erupted from your star with a force equal to a billion nuclear explosions. Its superheated particles are hitting your planet's atmosphere, each photon of light giving off a unique color as the storm heats the sky."

On the screen the colors dance and swirl, beautiful in their fury, as an icy-cold fear grips my heart.

"But my dad's up there—"

The sound of a shriek from inside the house spins me around. It sounds like a wild animal caught in a trap, but then I hear Mom screaming a single word.

"No!"

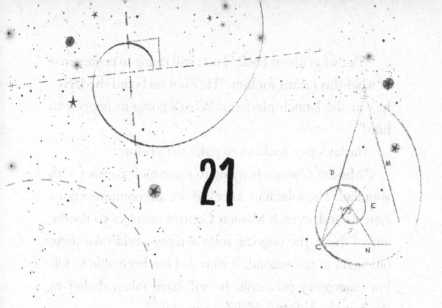

21

IN THE LIVING ROOM, MOM IS HOLDING CHARLIE IN HER ARMS as she rocks back and forth on the sofa. Granddad just sits there helplessly, holding his head in his bandaged hands as if trying to understand what Hayley's telling us.

"The solar flare caused catastrophic damage to the ISS's onboard computer systems. The Command and Control MDM, telemetry and communications interfaces, and life-support systems have all been fatally compromised. Failures in the electrical systems have caused multiple fires to break out in all sections of the space station, and its orbit is rapidly deteriorating. Mission Control has ordered the crew to evacuate using the docked Soyuz."

"But what about Dad?" I ask, still trying to make sense of what this means for him. "He's not on board the ISS—he's at the launch platform. What's going to happen to him?"

Hayley's face looks even paler than before.

"Mission Control is trying to reestablish contact with your dad. The solar flare knocked out all communications systems and, even if Mission Control manages to restore any of these, the ongoing solar activity could take them out again at any second. If your dad has been able to follow emergency protocols, he will have taken shelter in the launch platform's HabZone module."

I let out a sigh of relief, unaware until then that I'd been holding my breath for Hayley's reply.

"So he'll be safe there," I say.

Hayley hesitates. She glances down at Charlie, my sister's face a mask of puzzled tears as Mom holds her tight.

"Tell us," Mom pleads.

Hayley shakes her head, a tear running down her cheek.

"I'm sorry," she says. "Even if Dan managed to take shelter in the HabZone when the solar flare hit, we don't know whether any of his life-support systems have been compromised. If the HabZone is still pressurized, he's got a maximum of six hours of oxygen, but with the ISS falling out of orbit and the Soyuz evacuated, he's stranded there." Hayley's crying now, the words sputtering out. "There's no way to bring him back."

A black hole opens up inside me as Hayley's words sink in. I feel like I'm falling off the edge of the world, my thoughts reaching out in desperation for something to grab hold of, but there's nothing there. If Dad's alive, then he's trapped on the Lux Aeterna platform. Six hours of oxygen left and no spaceship to save him.

The black hole beats inside my chest.

It hurts so much.

From the TV comes a sudden burst of static, the blue screen replaced by a pixelated picture. For a second, I glimpse the bright white interior of the launch platform, the empty drawers of the Light Swarm delivery system still waiting for their payload. Then the picture disappears in another swarm of pixels, static buzzing from the speaker before the picture returns.

For a second I think this is the same blank blue screen as before, streaked now with white bands of interference, but then the picture shifts, and I see the curve of Earth and, beyond that, the darkness of space. The picture is framed by a rectangle of polished steel, and I realize that Dad's looking out from the HabZone observation window. The blue is the ocean, and the white bands of interference are clouds drifting above the surface of Earth.

Between the blue of Earth and the blackness of space,

I see rippling lights dancing across the horizon, curtains of green and gold enveloping the world in a rainbow embrace. It's just like Buzz showed me—the solar storm raging across the sky.

On the TV screen the angle shifts as Dad rests his helmet against the observation window. That's when I see it. The International Space Station silhouetted against the blue of the earth below. The familiar shape of its solar array is twisted out of recognition, jets of gas venting into space in multiple places from the damaged modules.

A growing cloud of debris is billowing behind the space station, and in the shade of this, I see the smaller shape of the Soyuz capsule, its main engine firing just like Dad said it would as it prepares for reentry. The last lifeboat leaving as the ISS burns. And Dad's not on board.

Tears are running down my face, Mom's sobs echoed by Charlie's wails. I can't imagine what Dad must be thinking right now.

There's a hiss of static, and then I hear the crackle of Dad's voice from the TV speakers.

"—like the ISS has suffered catastrophic damage. I hope everyone got out of there okay."

At the sound of Dad's voice, the black hole of my heart hammers even harder.

"I don't know if you guys at Mission Control can

even hear me now," Dad says. "But thanks to some kind of miracle, it looks like the Lux Aeterna systems are still fully operational, so I'm going to complete my mission and launch the Light Swarm probes."

There's another burst of static—the picture on the screen freezing and pixelating before sputtering back into life. I can see the banked units of the Light Swarm delivery system, the sleek white drawers still waiting for their cargo.

"—tell Jamie and Charlie that I love them and I'm sorry I couldn't make it home."

I hear a sudden hiss as Dad releases the catch on his helmet. Reaching up, he lifts it off his head and then turns the helmet to face him.

On the TV screen I see Dad looking back at me. His dark bangs are slicked to his forehead, his face drenched in sweat as he stares down the lens of his helmet camera.

I watch as Dad places his hand against the visor of the helmet.

"Bye, Jamie," he says, his words echoing across space. "I love you, son."

Then his voice is cut off by another burst of static as the picture on the screen freezes for the final time.

With a sob, I run toward the TV, pressing my hand against the screen as if I can just reach out and pull Dad through. But then the frozen image of Dad's hand disintegrates, the colored pixels collapsing into a blank blue screen as a dead dial tone rings out.

I turn around to see Mom holding Charlie tight, their faces stained with tears just like mine.

"He's gone."

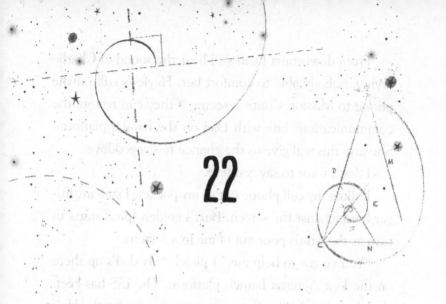

22

BIG BEN LIES TOPPLED, THE ORNATE DOME OF THE TAJ MAHAL
crushed to smithereens. The White House, the Eiffel
Tower, Brandenburg Gate—all shattered into hundreds
of pieces, just like they've been blown to bits at the start
of some sci-fi film.

I slump against the bed, my knees drawn up to my
chest as I try to control my tears.

The Lego models lie where they landed. The land-
marks of the world all turned to ruins with a swipe of my
arm as I swept them from the shelf above my bed. No
chance of Dad helping me to finish building them now.

Everything's ruined.

From downstairs I can still hear the sound of Charlie crying, nobody able to comfort her. Hayley's still on the phone to Mission Control, seeing if they can restore the communications link with Dad on the launch platform. She says this will give us the chance to say goodbye.

I don't want to say goodbye.

Pulling my cell phone out of my pocket, I stab my finger hard against the screen. Buzz's golden spiral starts to turn as the words pour out of me in a torrent.

"You've got to help me," I plead. "My dad's up there on the Lux Aeterna launch platform. The ISS has been abandoned, and the Soyuz is returning to Earth. He's stranded there in space, and there's no way to bring him back. Mission Control can't even reach him anymore. He's only got six hours of oxyg—"

"Hush." Buzz's voice cuts me off midflow. "Show me."

Hovering above the phone screen, the tip of my finger suddenly glows with a golden light. A strange tingling sensation washes over me as Buzz's words vibrate in my mind.

"Synchronizing."

On the screen the golden spiral fades to be replaced by a brand-new picture. I see Dad staring back at me, his face drenched in sweat. The black hole inside my chest aches as I watch his gloved hand reaching out to me.

For a second I think Buzz has managed to restore the communications link with the Lux Aeterna platform.

Then the picture on the screen disintegrates into a blur of colored pixels, and I realize that this is just a memory.

But instead of the pixels fading to be replaced by a blank blue screen, new images now flicker to life on my phone.

I see Dad dressed in his astronaut's suit at the Baikonur Cosmodrome, waiting to board the Soyuz rocket that will blast off for the ISS at the start of his mission. He's on the other side of the quarantine window, holding his hand up against the glass that separates us as I press my hand back against his. I'm not just seeing these images, it's like I'm reliving the emotions too—feeling the ache inside my heart as I wave goodbye to Dad.

The buzzing vibration inside my brain seems to quicken as Buzz riffles through my memories, their images filling the screen.

I see Dad sitting on my bedroom floor as we build the Taj Mahal together, Dad smiling as I slot the final Lego brick into place in the dome. Then I'm riding alongside him on Space Mountain at Disney World, the blue-white flashing lights illuminating Dad's grin as the roller coaster swoops into the blackness of space. I remember his arm slung around my shoulder, holding me tight as we barrel around another bend.

The images are speeding up as the memories reach back further in time.

The picture wobbles as on the screen. I glance back

over my shoulder to see Dad's proud expression as I pedal furiously. I remember this moment now. The first time I ever rode my bike without stabilizers. Then the picture shifts, and I'm looking up at my dad, his face younger now as he smiles encouragingly. The picture on the screen wobbles again as I take my first faltering steps, Dad's hands held out ready to catch me.

I didn't think I could remember these things, but as the images flit across the screen of my phone, I remember everything.

A blurry image appears on the screen before the picture sharpens to show a tiny hand. This looks like it belongs to a baby and, as I look at it, I realize that it's mine. Dad's face swims into view, his features even younger than before.

"Hey, Jamie," he says, his voice soft and gentle. On the screen Dad reaches out his hand, his fingers tracing the shape of my tiny fingers as he gently touches his hand to mine.

Then the picture slowly fades to black.

I can't stop myself from crying, my tears splashing onto the cell phone as Buzz's golden spiral fills the screen.

"Why did you show me this? It hurts too much."

"You are connected."

"Of course we're connected!" I cry, a sudden jet of anger erupting from the black hole inside me. "He's my dad! You don't know what this means—you're not even real anymore."

For a second there's silence, then my phone gently vibrates.

"We—I understand," Buzz replies, the words almost too soft to hear. "The light inside you is the light that binds you. To bring him back, you must go into the light."

"What do you mean?" I ask, my thoughts flickering between hope and fear.

"Inside the atoms of your body is a library of instructions," Buzz replies. "When you step into the light, the photons that bind every atom of your being will be unleashed and beamed to the Lux Aeterna platform."

"You're talking about teleportation?" I say, almost unable to believe that this could be possible. "Like on *Star Trek*?"

"Your star will guide you, but it will transform you too."

On the screen of my phone, a picture of the sun appears—the same sun I can see outside my bedroom window.

"You must go into the light," Buzz repeats as sunlight flares on the screen. "And then you will swarm."

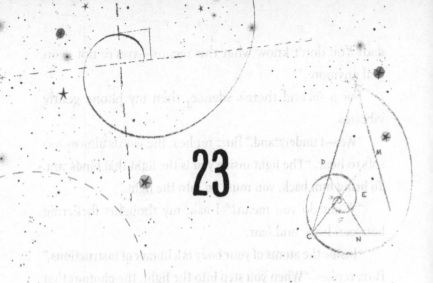

23

"I'M SO SORRY, JAMIE."

Brushing a braid of black hair from her face, Professor Forster wipes a tear from her eye.

"Shouldn't you be at home with your family now?"

I shake my head, the tears on my own face now dry. Looking up, I see the huge telescope towering above the astronomer's head as she sits at her desk.

"I need to use your telescope," I tell her. "It's the only chance I have to save my dad."

Professor Forster frowns.

"Jamie—I know you're upset, but you're not making any sense. You can't use a telescope in broad daylight."

My fingers tighten around my cell phone.

"I've got to look at the sun," I say, my voice cracking as I try to make Professor Forster understand. "Buzz told me . . ."

At the mention of Buzz's name, Professor Forster's frown deepens, her tearful expression now changing to a look of real concern.

"Jamie, I don't know how to tell you this, but I've been looking for the source of your 'alien' signal. I've gone back through the records and found a seven-second gap in the data feed when Hubble was studying the region of space surrounding Zeta Sagittarii. That must have been the moment when you plugged your phone into my laptop. Today I surveyed the same region of space to pinpoint the source of the transmission you think you received, but I couldn't find any signal. No stars, no extrasolar planets, no moons—no sign of alien life, intelligent or otherwise. I really wanted to believe it was true, but it can't be. There's nothing there, Jamie."

I don't have time for this. I *know* that Buzz is real.

"You're wrong," I say, thumping my phone down on the desk. In response, a pile of books topples across the table, and as these fall, I snatch the topmost book, the cover of which is filled with constellations. "I've seen the Hi'ive's home planet—there are two suns in the sky." I wave the copy of *The Stargazer's Guide* in the astronomer's face.

"Hubble must have made a mistake. Buzz is real. You've got to believe me."

On the desk between us, my cell phone buzzes, and glancing down, I see the spiral starting to spin.

"The black star came without warning." Buzz's voice vibrates in the silence of the observatory. "We had tamed our own stars, harvesting their energy to build a perfect world. No war, no hunger, no hatred. The Hi'ive lived as one in complete harmony. Our golden age lasted for more than five billion of your years. And then the black star came."

The screen of my phone suddenly turns purple as the image of an alien sky flickers to life there. Two suns shine in high definition, and we watch as these are slowly torn to pieces by an invisible hand.

Professor Forster stares at the phone openmouthed as Buzz continues to speak.

"We thought we had more time. The Hi'ive would go into the light and then swarm across the galaxy in search of a new home."

On the screen the picture shifts, and we now see a swarm of the strange alien creatures spiraling toward a golden light, their silvery wings beating to the sound of a buzzing prayer as the light surrounds them.

"Brothers and sisters, fathers and mothers—we all went into the light."

The light that fills the screen now is a star—a sun just like ours—but this star is being destroyed by a black hole. We watch as this golden light is shredded into blazing jets of gas and slowly devoured until only darkness remains.

"I cannot hear their voices anymore. All that is left is me." Buzz's words echo with an empty loneliness. "I am the Hi'ive."

Now I know why Buzz said he understood. I'm scared of losing my dad, but Buzz has lost everything.

"This is incredible," Professor Forster murmurs as Buzz's voice trails into silence. "An alien intelligence that has transformed from its biological form into a being of pure energy. These photons of light crossing the galaxy to escape a black hole until they hit the Hubble Space Telescope and were downloaded to your phone." She looks up at me, her eyes filled with wonder. "I'm so sorry I didn't believe you, Jamie."

"It doesn't matter," I reply, pointing toward the roof of the observatory. "I just need you to help me."

The astronomer's gaze rises to the telescope that towers above us. The hatch in the observatory roof is currently closed, the giant lens of the telescope staring not at the sun but at a rectangle of rust.

"But how?" Professor Forster scratches her head. "The solar flare that stranded your dad in space has already done its damage. Even if the telescope spots another solar storm on the way, this still won't help to bring back your dad."

I open my mouth, but before I can answer, Buzz's voice fills the room.

"We can harness the power of your star inside this observatory. To bring back his dad, Jamie must step into the light."

And then Buzz tells us what we need to do.

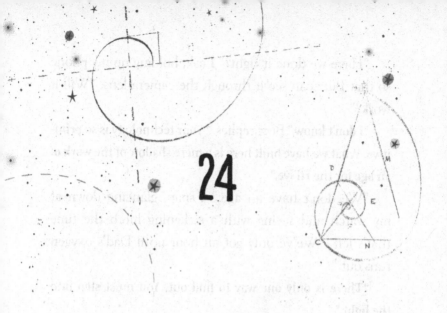

24

STEPPING BACK, I TAKE A FINAL LOOK AT THE MAKESHIFT
structure that we've built at the base of the telescope.
Wooden panels and metal shelves from the cabinets that
housed the computer equipment are stacked, seemingly
haphazardly, to make what looks like a tepee.

Glancing through the opening at the front, I can see
reels of magnetic tape draped in spiraling curtains, hiding
the interior from view. Professor Forster has cannibalized
the mobile Laser Optical Ground Station, following Buzz's
instructions to patch its electronics into the heart of the
structure. Multicolored cables twist around the outside,
humming with an untapped power as the frame rises to
meet the eye of the telescope.

"Have we done it right?" I ask, holding up my phone so that Buzz can see it through the camera lens. "Will it work?"

"I don't know," Buzz replies. "Your technology is so primitive. What we have built here is a mere shadow of the work of an age for the Hi'ive."

"We don't have an age," I snap, glancing down at my watch and seeing with a sickening lurch the time that's left. "We've only got an hour until Dad's oxygen runs out."

"There is only one way to find out. You must step into the light."

"Then let's do it," I say, desperate to get on with the job of saving my dad. I turn toward Professor Forster. "Open the hatch."

Standing by the observatory controls, the astronomer looks torn.

"I don't think you should do this, Jamie. It's too dangerous. If you look at the sun through a telescope, you'll go blind, but if you step inside this, you'll be torn to pieces." I can hear the fear in her voice. "There are seven trillion billion atoms inside your body. Even if the Hi'ive can teleport and reassemble them all on board the Lux Aeterna platform, there's no transporter room there to bring you back."

I look at the ramshackle tepee—a far cry from any

Star Trek invention. I can feel the black hole beating inside my chest. I don't care how dangerous it is—I've got to bring my dad home.

I glance down at the phone in my hand. Buzz has reprogrammed the ISS tracker app to fix on the location of the launch platform, while Professor Forster has connected my cell phone to the observatory's Wi-Fi. I'm running out of time, so I ask Buzz the only question that matters now.

"There's no way I could build anything like this up in space. How am I supposed to get back?"

"The light will be inside you," Buzz replies. **"That is all you need."**

I don't really understand what Buzz means, but as my watch ticks, there's no time to ask anything else. I call out again to Professor Forster.

"Please," I beg. "Open the hatch."

With a reluctant shake of her head, the astronomer presses a button to open the hatch in the roof of the dome. The telescope is already aimed straight at the sun, and, as the hatch slowly opens, daylight floods into the observatory.

At the base of the telescope the makeshift structure is enveloped in a golden glow. Its surface crackles with untamed energy as an intense buzzing sound fills the observatory.

Taking a faltering step forward, I peer fearfully into its interior. All I can see is a blinding white light.

"You can't do this, Jamie!" Professor Forster shouts, raising her voice above the deafening hum. "You'll be killed!"

Clutching my cell phone tightly, I shake my head.

"My dad's up there," I say, fighting against every urge that's telling me to turn and run. "And I'm going to find him."

I step forward into the light, the buzzing noise silenced as the light surrounds me.

And then I swarm.

166

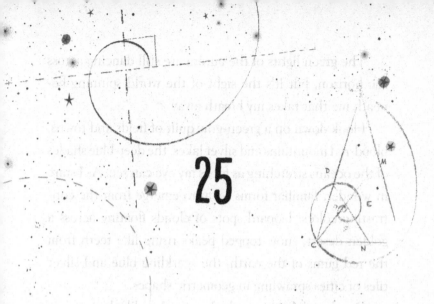

25

I DON'T KNOW WHICH WAY IS UP. THE LIGHT SURROUNDS
me—inside and out—red, orange, yellow, green, blue,
violet. I'm floating in an ocean of color, the light waves
shimmering in perfect silence.

My mind tries to make sense of what's happening to
me. People who've nearly died say they go toward the
light. Is *this* what death feels like? Am I still alive?

I try to blink, a single flicker of my eyelids seeming to
last for an eternity.

I open my eyes to see the blackness of space, the darkness studded with thousands of stars. And stretching out
below this, I can see the curve of Earth.

The green lights of the aurora are still dancing across the horizon, but it's the sight of the world spinning beneath me that takes my breath away.

I look down on a green-gray quilt of fields and towns, blood-red mountains and silver lakes, the deep blue shades of the oceans stretching as far as my eye can see. As I stare in wonder, familiar forms seem to emerge from the contrasting colors: leopard spots of clouds floating across a golden desert, snow-topped peaks rising like teeth from the red gums of the earth, the sparkling blue and silver tiles of cities sprawling in geometric shapes.

On the globe in my bedroom, thin black lines are drawn to mark the shapes of the different countries, but from up here, these lines are invisible. No borders, no countries—just one world rolling by beneath me.

It's so beautiful.

A tear creeps out of the corner of my eye. Instead of rolling down my cheek, this tiny ball of liquid hangs suspended, pooling in the corner of my eye.

According to Mrs. Solomon, there are seven and a half billion people alive in the world today. And they're all down there. All my friends, all my family, everyone I've ever met, everyone I've ever watched on TV, everyone I love—Mom, Charlie, Granddad—everyone except one person.

Pushing myself away from the observation window, I

spin around. As I float weightlessly, my eyes slowly adjust to the bright interior of the launch platform. And that's when I see Dad.

He's standing in front of the Light Swarm delivery system, all of its drawers now fully loaded, except one. In the palm of Dad's hand, I see the diamond shape of the final Light Swarm probe.

Calling out his name, I push myself forward, soaring through the empty air toward him. My mind whirls as my stomach flips, the sensation dizzying.

I'm flying like a superhero. I'm going to save my dad.

I keep waiting for him to turn around, but Dad just stays frozen, motionless. The black hole thuds inside my chest. I reach out my hands to stop myself from flying straight past Dad, one hand still holding onto my phone.

Grabbing hold of the edge of the Light Swarm delivery system, I come to a stop with a sickening lurch, spinning around until I'm facing Dad.

His head is bent over the Light Swarm probe, the expression on his face set in a picture of concentration as he prepares to slide the black chip into the nano-spacecraft. He looks just like he does when he reads the instructions on my Lego kits, making sure we've got all the pieces sorted before we start the build. I brush the tear from my eye, this tiny ball of liquid floating free in front of me.

"Dad," I say again, waiting for him to lift his head

and see me there. "It's me—Jamie. I've come to take you home."

But Dad's eyes stay fixed on the Light Swarm probe, his expression unchanged.

I hold up my cell phone, my hand glowing with the same golden light that spirals on the home screen.

"What's the matter with my dad?" I plead. "Why can't he hear me?"

Buzz's voice hums in my ear.

"You are traveling at the speed of light," Buzz replies. **"Every atom of your being is vibrating at 299,792,458 meters per second as the light inside you swarms. Time is dilated. For you, your dad appears to be frozen as you see time passing infinitely more slowly for him. You only have a moment—a lifetime—before the light inside you returns to its source."**

My brain hurts as I try to wrap my head around Buzz's explanation. Nothing makes any sense to me. Buzz is a super-advanced alien intelligence, and I'm just a kid.

Floating in space, I stare helplessly at my dad. I feel as though there's a glass screen between us—just like there was when Dad was in quarantine. How can I break through this to bring him home?

As if hearing this last unspoken word, Buzz's voice echoes around the HabZone.

"When we went into the light, the Hi'ive hoped that we would find a new home. Light is eternal. From the moment

170

of its birth, a single photon can travel endlessly across the universe. Never decaying, never dying, until it reaches its final destination and is reflected or absorbed. We thought this would give us the greatest chance of survival. But now I am trapped inside this small primitive machine."

I can hear the sadness in Buzz's voice, a cosmic loneliness that seems to ache for the stars. I look at the Light Swarm probe in the palm of Dad's hand and suddenly know what I've got to do.

Flipping the phone over, I snap open the back of the case. Next to the battery, I see the phone's SD card nestling in its holder. That's where Buzz is now.

"What are you doing?" Buzz asks as I struggle to pry it out.

"Setting you free," I reply. "The Light Swarm probes are being launched for Tau Ceti—a star twelve light-years away from Earth. If you hitch a ride, maybe you can find a new home there—a place for the Hi'ive to start again."

"A new home . . ." Buzz falls silent for a moment as if staring out into the star-studded sky. "We—I would like that. Thank you, Jamie."

Outside the window the world keeps turning. Earth was formed about four and a half billion years ago. The human race has lived on this planet for maybe two hundred thousand years. In that time we've discovered fire, invented the wheel, built pyramids, written books, made music, and created the Internet. Dad has flown into space to launch our first spaceships for the stars. The Hi'ive have lived for so much longer than us, but their greatest achievement is floating in front of me. Buzz has given me back my dad.

"Thank you."

Inside my head, I feel a strange buzzing vibration, and as I look down at my hands, I see the light start to shine through. I don't have much time.

Sliding the SD card out from my phone, I reach out to take the Light Swarm probe. As my fingers brush against Dad's hand, I feel the vibration inside me start to quicken—the two of us separated by the speed of light.

Trying to ignore this, I slide the SD card into the heart of the Light Swarm probe. It fits perfectly. Then I load the probe into the final empty drawer of the delivery system, ready to launch Buzz to the stars.

On the control panel, there's a large red button that reads ACTIVATE LAUNCH SEQUENCE.

The humming sound inside my head sharpens to a high-pitched whine. Buzz said I had a moment—a lifetime—but it looks like this is almost over. . . .

I feel myself starting to unravel, the photons of light that are holding me together slowly being tugged apart. With a desperate lunge, I push the red button as spidery beams of light start to vent from my fingers.

Above the buzzing noise, I hear a hydraulic hiss that tells me that the Light Swarm probes are launching. I've done it. I've given Buzz the chance to survive, but I think it might be too late for me.

I'm falling to pieces, my body collapsing into light itself, and there's only one person who can save me. Turning toward Dad, I wrap my arms around him, burying my face in the folds of his bulky space suit.

I thought that I'd lost him forever, but as I hold Dad tightly, the black hole inside me is transformed into a shining star. I hear his voice soft in my ear.

"Jamie."

The star suddenly bursts into supernova. A brilliant light brighter than the entire galaxy surrounds us, and then we're gone.

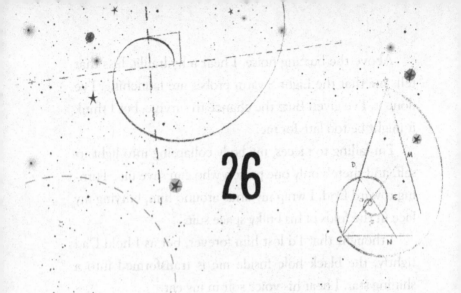

26

I FOLLOW THE NEW PATH THAT LEADS TO THE TOP OF BEACON Hill, a carpet of stars glittering beneath my feet as darkness falls. Emerging from the trees, I first see the white dome of the observatory, now scrubbed clean, ready for its grand reopening. But it's the sight of Mom's sculpture that makes me gasp in surprise.

Four curving columns made out of glass and steel rise up in front of the observatory. The moon overhead fills these with light, their colored glass a shimmering beacon in the darkness.

"Race you to Mom's swirly thing!" Charlie shouts, running past me with a delighted squeal. With a grin I

174

start to chase my little sister, following the twisting path as it heads up the hill.

As I run, I keep my eyes fixed on Mom's sculpture. At first the four columns stand alone, but as the path curves around, the position of the pillars seems to shift, the curling shapes slotting together to form a shimmering spiral reaching up into the night sky.

I glance over my shoulder to where Mom and Dad are walking along the path, the two of them laughing together as they watch Charlie and me race for the top.

They're still getting divorced, even though I kind of hoped that everything that happened with Dad would push them back together. But it's like Mom and Dad told Charlie and me—just because they're splitting up doesn't mean we're not a family anymore. We're just one that has a different shape now—a bit like Mom's sculpture. And we can still come together on a night like this.

Inside the observatory, Professor Forster will be getting everything ready. Dad's the guest of honor who will cut the ribbon and declare the Beacon Hill Observatory open to the public.

Nobody really knows how he made it home from the Lux Aeterna platform. Mission Control invented a story about Dad making his escape in an emergency Soyuz module once he'd launched the Light Swarm probes. Only Professor Forster really knows what happened. She was there waiting for us inside the observatory when we fell to Earth, my arms wrapped around Dad as we stepped out of the light.

The European Space Agency, NASA, and Roscosmos—the Russian State Corporation for Space Activities—launched a joint top-secret investigation to find out the truth. Dad and I were interviewed tons of times in confidential debriefings, everyone wanting to know how he ended up sitting with me on top of Beacon Hill as the oxygen on the Lux Aeterna platform ran out.

I just told them the truth.

An alien on my phone helped me bring Dad home.

They didn't believe me, but the space agency investigators still took my cell phone away. It's probably in tiny pieces now, but they won't find a trace of the Hi'ive. Buzz is long gone—traveling at near light speed on a one-way trip to Tau Ceti.

I hope he makes it.

Professor Forster calls Buzz the one that got away. At first I thought she was going to be angry that I'd let proof that aliens exist just disappear into the depths of space, but she said she doesn't mind. She told me it's enough to know that we found them at last. And with Dad's help she's reopened the observatory to the public so that everyone can learn more about the universe.

Dad believes me. We're making a model of the Hi'ive's

176

home planet out of Lego bricks, based on everything I can remember. And this time we're going to finish it.

Charlie's nearly at the sculpture now. I hang back for a second to let her win the race, then dash to catch her as she runs inside the spiral. My sister shrieks with delight as I scoop her up into my arms. I whirl Charlie around, moonlit rainbows dancing across our faces as we gaze up at the stars.

There are thousands of them, twinkling in the darkness.

"Look at all the lights," Charlie says, her voice squeaky with excitement.

I used to think Dad was the star of our family's solar system, but now I know that the light shines in all of us. Buzz showed me that. Sometimes things go wrong and we might spin out of orbit, but we need to remember that we're not alone. We get this one brief moment in the sun, and if you're lucky enough to fill yours with love, let it shine.

Mom and Dad join us in the heart of the sculpture, Dad slipping his arm around my shoulder as Mom takes Charlie in her arms. For a second, we stand there in silence, all troubles forgotten as we stare in wonder at the stars.

THE SCIENCE OF
THE JAMIE DRAKE EQUATION

From wafer-sized spaceships to the extraterrestrial Wow! signal, here's more about the real-life science in *The Jamie Drake Equation*.

Aliens don't really exist, do they?

You do the math. In our solar system, there are eight planets orbiting the Sun, but only one where we know that intelligent life exists, and that's our own—planet Earth. But our galaxy, the Milky Way, contains more than two hundred billion stars, and the Milky Way is only one of hundreds of billions of galaxies that make up the universe. That's why astronomer Frank Drake devised the Drake Equation in 1961 to try to estimate how many intelligent extraterrestrial civilizations there could be in our galaxy.

$$N = R^* \times f_p \times n_e \times f_l \times f_i \times f_c \times L$$

In the Drake Equation, N is the number of alien civilizations we might be able to receive signals from. To work out the value of N, Frank Drake said you'd need to estimate the rate at which stars that could support life are being formed in our galaxy (R^*); what fraction of these stars will have planets (f_p); how many of those planets could potentially support life (n_e); the fraction of these planets that will actually develop life (f_l); the fraction of these planets that will develop intelligent life, i.e., alien civilizations (f_i); the fraction of these alien civilizations that will develop communications technologies capable of releasing signals into space (f_c); and how long these civilizations could send signals for (L). The numbers keep getting smaller as you move along the equation, and we have to guess the answer to all of them except the rate of star formation (R^*). But by plugging his best guesses into the equation, Frank Drake estimated that there could be as many as ten thousand alien civilizations in the Milky Way.

Ten thousand! Then why haven't we heard from any aliens yet?

This question is known as the Fermi paradox and is named after the physicist Enrico Fermi. One day when Fermi was discussing with other scientists the possibility that there are many intelligent alien civilizations out there in our galaxy, with many of them more advanced than our own, he asked the simple question "Where are they?" We have no evidence of the existence of alien life, even though the chance that it exists in our galaxy seems so high. Many people have come up with explanations for the Fermi paradox. One is that space is so big that an alien civilization might be too far away for us to contact; another suggests that Earth is being kept in some kind of cosmic zoo with aliens studying us but keeping their own existence a secret!

But what about the Wow! signal? Couldn't that have been aliens trying to get in touch?

Since the 1960s, scientists have been using radio telescopes to scour the skies in search of alien signals. This is known as the search for extraterrestrial intelligence (SETI) and, in 1977, astronomers at the Big Ear Observatory at Ohio University detected an unusually strong 72-second radio signal from the direction of the star Tau Sagittarii. In addition to its intensity, which made the astronomer who first noticed it scribble the word "Wow!" next to a printout of the radio pulse, there was something else about this signal that made scientists sit up and listen. The signal was detected at the 1420 megahertz radio frequency, which is a wavelength of 21 centimeters. The most common chemical element in the universe is hydrogen, and hydrogen atoms emit radio waves at this exact same frequency. Many scientists believe that any alien civilizations who wanted the signals they were sending into space to be detected would use this same frequency, as they'd realize that another intelligent civilization who could detect radio waves would tune their telescopes to the frequency of hydrogen to find out more about the universe. This is why astronomers got so excited when they detected the Wow! signal. Unfortunately, no further similar radio signal has ever been detected from this area of space. So the jury's still out about whether this signal was aliens trying to get in touch!

But if we're just listening to radio waves, how will we know if the signals we detect come from an alien civilization?

Any signal we receive from an extraterrestrial civilization isn't going to be transmitted in any language we speak here on Earth. However, some scientists think that an intelligent alien civilization might use a language that would be understood all across the universe: the language of mathematics.

If you think mathematics is a universal language, then you haven't seen my school report card. . . .

Don't worry. It's unlikely that E.T. will be sending the human race a math quiz across the galaxy. However, a more advanced extraterrestrial civilization would be likely to have the same fundamental mathematical knowledge that we have worked out as the human race. If scientists detected a signal that transmitted radio pulses in bursts that match the Fibonacci sequence or another common mathematical series of numbers, they would have evidence that the sender of the signal was intelligent. Some scientists think that an advanced alien civilization might even be able to encode information in any signals they send. So one day, if we do detect an alien transmission, we might be able to download a selfie E.T. has sent us!

So we've just got to wait for aliens to get in touch?

Scientists aren't just sitting around waiting for evidence of alien life to land in their laps. The search for extraterrestrial intelligence is using lots of different tools: radio telescopes scan the skies for alien transmissions, and other kinds of telescopes search for extrasolar planets. By analyzing the light emitted by a star, astronomers can determine whether any planets are in orbit around it, and even the distance at which they're orbiting. This information in turn helps astronomers determine whether any planets they detect are in the Goldilocks zone, the habitable zone around a star where surface water—and life—has a chance of existing. In the book, Jamie's dad, Commander Dan Drake, is sending the Light Swarm probes to Tau

Ceti to search for evidence of alien life. In the real world, scientists have detected two extrasolar planets in orbit in the habitable zone around this star.

But the Light Swarm probes are just science fiction, right? We can't really send tiny spaceships the size of an SD card into space, can we?

Not yet, but world-famous scientist Professor Stephen Hawking has teamed up with Facebook founder Mark Zuckerberg and other wealthy investors to develop Breakthrough Starshot. This research and engineering project aims to develop nanotechnology and powerful lasers to launch ultralight postage stamp–sized space probes to the nearby star of Alpha Centauri, which is just over four light-years away. These tiny spaceships would be equipped with a sail, which would catch the laser beam and then be accelerated to 25 percent of the speed of light. Traveling at up to 100 million miles an hour, these probes could reach Alpha Centauri in approximately twenty years and then beam pictures of what they find there to us back here on Earth. So if Breakthrough Starshot is a success, maybe one day we'll discover whether aliens really exist. . . .

ACKNOWLEDGMENTS

Writing fiction sometimes feels like setting off on an interstellar journey into the unknown, but I'd like to think my wonderful editor, Kirsty Stansfield, and my brilliant agent, Lucy Juckes, for helping to guide me on this journey with their wise words of counsel from Mission Control. Thank you too to Fiona, Dom, Catherine, Kitty, Kate, Ola, Tom, and all the team at Nosy Crow.

Huge thanks to Dr. Elizabeth Pearson and Professor Dan Tovey for their invaluable scientific advice and astronomical guidance. Any scientific errors and exaggerations remaining in the text are, of course, my own. I'd also like to thank the authors of the following books for helping to light the way as I researched all things astronomical: *The Aliens Are Coming!* by Ben Miller, *An Astronaut's Guide to Life on Earth* by Colonel Chris Hadfield, *Human Universe* by Professor Brian Cox and Andrew Cohen, *Light Years* by Brian Clegg, and *An Astronomer's Tale* by Gary Fildes.

The interstellar ambition of the fictional Light Swarm mission is inspired by the exciting work of the Breakthrough Starshot Initiative, led by Professor Stephen Hawking and Yuri Milner and financed by Mark Zuckerberg. I'd also like to thank Tim Peake and his Principia Mission for inspiring a new generation to look at the stars and wonder.

Finally, I'd like to thank my family for all their love, support, and understanding, especially when I float off into worlds of my own imagining. You are my universe.

TURN THE PAGE FOR A PREVIEW
OF A UNIVERSE-HOPPING ADVENTURE
BY CHRISTOPHER EDGE. . . .

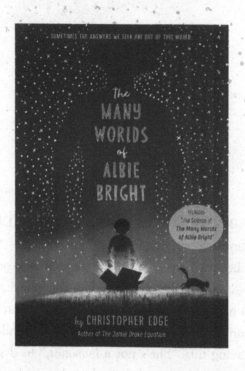

HOW FAR WOULD YOU GO TO CHANGE YOUR WORLD?

Fascinating science meets humor and heart in this story about a boy who is searching for his mother . . . in a parallel universe.

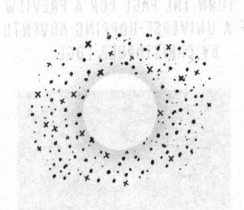

IT WAS MY DAD WHO GAVE ME THE IDEA OF using quantum physics to find my mum.

She died two weeks ago. Her funeral was on Tuesday. It was at St. Thomas's Church in the village. At first Dad said he wanted something called a humanist funeral without any "religious mumbo jumbo," but Granddad Joe wasn't having this. "She's not a *humanist*," he'd said, almost spitting out his tea when Dad tried to explain. "She's my daughter."

He said that Mum had been christened at St. Thomas's Church when she was a baby, and he wanted her ashes buried there too, right next to Grandma Joyce, looking out toward the wind turbines and the mine at the edge of the moors.

That's where Mum used to work—down in the pit. She wasn't a coal miner; she was a *scientist*. You see, Clackthorpe Pit is one of the deepest mines in Great Britain, and when the coal ran out, it was scientists searching for the secrets of the universe who moved in there instead. Down at the bottom of the mine, they could use all their high-tech equipment without any cosmic rays interfering with their experiments.

Cosmic rays are radiation from outer space. Every second of the day, dozens of these cosmic rays zip through your body and you don't even notice a thing. Don't worry, they won't turn you into a bug-eyed mutant, but they can seriously mess up the kind of experiments Mum and Dad do, so that's why they've got to hide them away underground.

Mum and Dad used to joke that their first date was a thousand meters beneath the moors. They went down into the mine looking for dark matter—the invisible glue that sticks the universe together—and found each other instead. They got married, and (skipping the embarrassing biology bit) eight months later I showed up. Albert Stephen Bright. I was named after Mum and Dad's favorite scientists, Albert Einstein and Stephen Hawking, but everyone calls me Albie for short.

According to my mum, my early arrival was a bit like the big bang—a complete surprise, and pretty scary too—and I ended up staying in the hospital until I was nearly four months old. Then, when I finally got better, Mum and Dad took me with them when they went to work at CERN in Switzerland.

CERN is like Disneyland for scientists. It's where the World Wide Web was invented, and now it's the home of the Large Hadron Collider. In case you haven't seen it on TV, the Large Hadron Collider is the biggest machine in the world. It's sixteen and a half miles long and weighs a whopping 38,000 tons. That's why it's called the *Large* Hadron Collider. Scientists built the LHC to look inside the smallest things in the universe: atoms.

Everything in the universe is made out of atoms— you, me, this piece of paper, even the sun. And the thing about atoms is they're small—very small. To give you an idea of how incredibly tiny I'm talking here, take a look at the period at the end of this sentence. Had a good look? Now, that period has eight trillion atoms inside it. That's 8,000,000,000,000 atoms. Count those zeroes. There are more atoms in that period than there are people alive in the world today. That's pretty amazing, don't you think? And every atom is made up of even smaller particles called protons, neutrons, and electrons.

When I asked Mum why she needed such a big machine to look inside something so small, she told me that the Large Hadron Collider is like an underground race-track for atoms, but the winner is the one who has the biggest crash. In the collider, these tiny particles race around and around in circles, getting faster and faster until they smash together at almost the speed of light. Mum said this creates a mini big bang—a bit like the one that made the universe—and by studying this, Mum and Dad hoped to find out exactly how everything began.

There was just one problem. In addition to those mini big bangs, it turned out that smashing atoms together at nearly the speed of light might make mini black holes too. A black hole is like an invisible vacuum cleaner in outer space, sucking up anything that gets too close. This book my dad wrote says that the gravity inside a black hole is so strong that not even light can escape. If you tried to fly a spaceship past for a closer look, you'd get sucked inside the black hole and turned into spaghetti.

Of course, the idea of the Large Hadron Collider creating a black hole here on Earth wasn't that popular. Before you knew it, TV news crews from around the world were turning up at CERN to accuse Mum, Dad, and the rest of the scientists there of plotting to DESTROY THE WORLD! It ended up being my dad who was pushed in front of the TV cameras to explain how this was totally ridiculous and that any black holes that *were* created inside the collider would evaporate instantly without Earth being sucked inside out.

That's when he got discovered by a talent scout. A TV company offered Dad the chance to make his own series,

Ben Bright's Guide to the Universe: Everything You Ever Wanted to Know About Space for People Who Hated Science at School. It turned out that quite a lot of people hated science at school, because eight million people ended up watching. One TV reviewer even nicknamed my dad The Man Who Can Explain Everything, but to be honest, he wasn't much help with my homework. Most of the time he wasn't even home, since he was flying around the world filming cool science stuff for his next TV show.

Whenever Dad did turn up to collect me from school, I usually ended up hanging around waiting while my teachers took a selfie with him. It was seriously embarrassing, but Mum didn't seem to mind. She used to joke that all the time Dad spent being a TV star just gave her more time to get on with the real science, and that she'd win a Nobel Prize before him.

That was before Mum got the news that changed everything.

In this mind-bending mystery, a girl must work with the laws of the universe and trust the love of her family if she is to set her world right.

The insistent beeping of my alarm clock pulls me out of a super weird dream. Something about talking dolphins and the end of the world, I think.

It's funny how that moment in a dream just before you wake up can seem like the most real moment there's ever been. You completely believe that it's true—that it's really happening to you—even if you are talking to a dolphin at the time. But then when you open your eyes, the dream starts to fade right away, and all that you're left with is a strange jumble of thoughts that don't seem to make any sense at all.

Fumbling for the button on top of my alarm clock,

I shake the last of the dream fragments from my mind, my eyes blinking in time with the numbers displayed on the digital screen.

9:00 a.m.

For a second I panic, wondering why nobody has tried to wake me up yet, but then I see the date.

SATURDAY, JUNE 9

It's my birthday.

Jumping down from my cabin bed, I pull open the curtains, and sunlight floods into my room. Through the window I can see the gazebo that Mom and Dad have bought for my birthday party laid out across the lawn beneath protective plastic sheets, just waiting now for Dad to put it up. Over the back fence I can see the railway tracks, and beyond that the backs of the shops that lead up Cheswick Hill, the whole scene bathed in perfect summer sunshine.

I can't stop myself from grinning. Today is going to be the best day ever. I'm ten years old.

The ancient Greek philosopher Pythagoras thought the number ten was the most important number in the world. He basically invented math using it and believed that the whole universe was built out of numbers. Pythagoras said that the number ten contained the key to understanding everything. If this is true, being ten years old is going to be pretty cool.

Maybe now that I'm ten, Mom and Dad will let me go to the shops on my own or even stay up late, just like Lily.

Lily's my older sister. She's fifteen and she hates me.

Mom and Dad say that Lily doesn't hate me. They say she's just a bit stressed at the moment because she's studying for her A-levels for university, but I don't think that's a very good excuse. I passed those exams when I was seven, getting a distinction in physics, chemistry, and math. Now I'm studying for a bachelor of science in mathematics and physics.

The thing is, I'm "academically gifted." Apparently this puts me in the top 2 percent of the population. That doesn't mean I'm smarter than everybody else. I'm absolutely terrible at French. I just love learning about how the universe works. Lily thinks this makes me a freak.

Like I said, she hates me.

Pulling on my robe over my pajamas, I head down the stairs. The house is so quiet. Usually Dad's already in the kitchen by now, noisily cooking up his Saturday-morning pancake breakfast while Mom sits at the kitchen table reading the newspaper.

I turn right at the bottom of the stairs, heading down

the hallway and into the kitchen. Beneath my bare feet, the black-and-white tiles covering the floor feel freezing cold. I shiver. The kitchen table is deserted, the frying pan standing silent as the empty counters gleam. There's nobody here.

I peer through the patio doors that lead out into the backyard, wondering for a second if Mom and Dad have sneaked out there to start putting up the gazebo for my party later today, but there's nobody there either.

Maybe they are hiding somewhere and are going to jump out any minute singing "Happy Birthday."

"Mom! Dad!" I call out. "Where are you?"

I stand still for a moment, ready to look all surprised when they suddenly appear. But nobody jumps out. The grin I've been wearing since I opened my bedroom curtains is slowly starting to fade. If Mom and Dad think this is funny, I've got news for them.

The living room is just as empty as the kitchen, the TV turned off and not a cushion out of place on the sofa. I'm not surprised that Lily's not up yet, as she doesn't usually surface until after ten on the weekend. This is because she's a teenager and the hormones in her brain make her sleep late. Maybe that will start happening to me now that I'm ten. Now that I'm ten, everything might change.

I've done a loop of the downstairs now: hall, kitchen, living room, and back to the hall. If Mom and Dad are hiding somewhere ready to give me a birthday surprise, then they're running out of rooms. Our house really isn't that big.

Standing at the bottom of the stairs, I call out again.

"Mom! Dad! This isn't funny. Where are you?"

Still no answer—just a creepy silence that seems to fill the house. I shiver, even though sunlight is streaming through the arch of tinted glass at the top of the front door behind me. Where is everyone? They wouldn't have gone out without me. The excitement I felt when I sprang out of bed has now turned into a nagging sense of worry. I race up the stairs, two steps at a time, wanting this stupid game of hide-and-seek to be over already.

Heading around the landing, I push open the door to Mom and Dad's bedroom.

The room is still in darkness, the curtains drawn against the morning sun, but in the light spilling in from the landing I can see that nobody's here. The bedspread is pulled neatly across Mom and Dad's king-size bed. It doesn't look like it's even been slept in.

The twisting worry that's been coiling inside my stomach is now tightening into a tense knot of fear.

Doubling back along the landing, I glance back inside my bedroom and then peer around the bathroom door too, just to double-check. But both rooms are empty. The only living thing I can see is a spider scurrying toward the faucets when I pull the shower curtain back.

I shiver again, the sunlight streaming through the

bathroom window seeming to lack any kind of warmth. Something's not right.

Back on the landing, I glance toward the second flight of stairs that lead up to Lily's room in the attic. A NO ENTRY sign is stuck to the wall at the bottom of the stairs, and beneath this Lily has written NO SISTERS ALLOWED.

She means me.

I wouldn't normally dare to go anywhere near Lily's room on a Saturday morning. Her rage can be positively volcanic if her weekend sleep is disturbed. But this isn't a normal Saturday. It's my birthday, and I want to know where everyone is.

"Lily!" I shout up the stairs, my words echoing off the empty walls. "Are you up yet?"

There's no answer.

"Lily?"

More silence.

I glance at the NO ENTRY sign and then shake my head. This is an emergency.

Taking a step forward, I start to climb the stairs. Inside my head, I quickly flick through the excuses I'll use when Lily freaks out at me for waking her up. I don't know what I'll do if she's not in her room.

Our house is usually filled with noise. This silence is really starting to get to me.

Then the doorbell rings.

I jump in surprise, but as soon as I realize what this means, a sudden wave of relief washes over me. This must be Mom and Dad. They must've got up early to get things ready for my party and then realized that they needed something from the shops. Leaving me and Lily in bed, they popped out and are now back with bagfuls of party stuff and need me to let them in.

I race back down the stairs, skipping around the landing and then barreling down the second flight of stairs. It's time to get my birthday started at last.

As I reach the hallway, the sound of the front doorbell seems to stretch out as if someone has left their finger on it for too long. Then it stops abruptly, and the air hums with absolute silence again.

It must be broken.

Feeling kind of puzzled, I fix a smile to my face, eager to find out exactly what Mom and Dad have got me from the shops.

But when I open the front door, this smile is suddenly eclipsed as my lips stretch wide in a silent scream. The sound of my cheery hello curdles in my throat as I look in horror at the scene outside.

There's nobody there.

But worse than that, there's nothing there.

No Mom. No Dad. No car parked in the driveway. No driveway. No street. No houses.

Nothing at all.